# MURDER, LIES AND CHOCOLATE

**Sally Berneathy**

*Best wishes*
*Sally B*

*Books by Sally Berneathy*

**Death by Chocolate**
(book 1 in the Death by Chocolate series)

**Murder, Lies and Chocolate**
(book 2 in the Death by Chocolate series)

**The Great Chocolate Scam**
(book 3 in the Death by Chocolate series)

**The Ex Who Wouldn't Die**
(book 1 in Charley's Ghost series)

**The Ex Who Glowed in the Dark**
(book 2 in Charley's Ghost series)

This book is a work of fiction. The names, characters, places and incidents are products of the writer's imagination or have been used fictitiously and are not to be construed as real. Any resemblance to persons, living or dead, or to actual events, locales or organizations is entirely coincidental (except for Fred and King Henry).

Murder, Lies and Chocolate
Copyright ©2012 Sally Berneathy

ISBN-10: 1939551080
ISBN-13: 978-1-939551-08-5

Original cover art by fellow author and friend, Bob Moats, http://murdernovels.com

# Chapter One

"Are you out of your freaking mind? No, you cannot have my house." I spoke the words through gritted teeth to keep myself from shouting since it was noon and my small restaurant, Death by Chocolate, was packed. I didn't want my customers to hear me screaming at my almost-ex-husband. Might ruin their appetite for dessert. I had no doubt Rick deliberately chose that setting so I wouldn't yell at him.

"Lindsay, you'd have to be crazy to pass up a deal like this." Rick leaned across the counter and gave me his most engaging, most insincere real estate salesman smile. "You'll get almost twice what that old place is worth, and I'll sign the divorce papers the minute you sign the Contract for Sale."

Rick knew how to work me. He'd convinced me to marry him in the first place and now he'd delayed our divorce for almost a year. Every time I got a court date, he got a continuance. I really, really wanted him to sign those papers and I certainly could have used the extra money, but I've learned not to trust a Rick bearing gifts. He was up to something. Had he discovered my house had oil under the basement? Was the railroad scheduled to come through? I was pretty sure those things only happened in old movies, but I was equally sure this deal would have some money in it for Rick, more than was in it for me.

"Do you not see that I'm busy right now? Go away." I turned to the man who'd taken a seat on the stool next to where Rick stood. "What can I get for you, sir? Our special today is a ham sandwich and a piece of Sinful Chocolate Cake."

"I'm not leaving," Rick said. "I'm meeting my client here. Throw a little business your way. We'll be at that table in the corner in case you change your mind. Give it some thought." He smiled and winked as he walked across the room.

Had I really once thought that smile was sexy?

Paula Roberts, my best friend and co-worker, was waiting tables while I took care of the counter. That meant she'd have to deal with him. Not that I wished Rick on her, but better her than me. At least he was a good tipper, especially when he was with a client. The old impress.

For the next hour I focused on serving sandwiches and chocolate goodies and tried to ignore Rick. I did notice that an older male joined him. Probably really was a real client. I'd expected him to bring in his latest bimbo. Excuse me...I mean, his latest girlfriend.

The man was likely the client who wanted to buy my house since he and Rick kept looking at me.

When Rick and I split up he moved his bimbo-of-the-month, Muffy, into the big home we once shared, and I moved into one of our small rental properties in the Kansas City suburb of Pleasant Grove. I wasn't happy about it at the time, but I'd since become quite fond of that house. It has character and personality as well as great neighbors. Paula and her son, Zach, live on one side with my OCD computer nerd friend, Fred Sommers, on the other.

True, with as much money as Rick was offering, I could buy the vacant house across the street and fix it up, thus retaining my neighbors. That was just one of the many reasons I didn't trust the whole deal. Why would anybody offer that much more than the house was worth? I did not for one minute believe Rick's story that his client's grandparents had lived in the house and he wanted it for sentimental value. What a crock.

The lunch crowd began to thin, and I noticed Rick and his client still sitting at the corner table. Across the room Paula cleared the dirty dishes off the table next to them and exchanged a raised-eyebrow look with me. I repressed a sigh as I handed the last lady at the bar a to-go bag with half a dozen gluten-free chocolate chip cookies. Rick was obviously planning to wait until everybody was gone then ambush me. He didn't like not getting his way. That's why our divorce was still pending. He didn't want it, and if he didn't want something, he'd figure a way to stop that something from happening.

A few months before he had kicked Muffy out and decided he wanted me back in. By that time I'd recovered from the temporary insanity that had induced me to marry him in the first place and got a cat instead. That cat loves my house. Make that, *our* house. King Henry took ownership the day he moved in.

The last customer left the counter. Besides Rick and his buddy, only one other table remained occupied. An older man and a younger woman sat there, nibbling on their cookies, talking softly and laughing. Probably married but not to each other.

Paula took her load of dishes to the kitchen then returned to where I stood behind the cash register. After her evil ex-husband was sent to prison last fall, she quit coloring her blonde hair brown and came out of hiding, but she still wore her self-appointed uniform of long sleeves and ankle-length skirts to hide the scars he'd left. I'd worn the same uniform for a while to make her feel comfortable but had recently gone back to jeans and white shirts. I'd tripped on those long skirts too many times.

"They didn't order anything except desert, and Rick gave me a twenty dollar tip," she said. "Watch your back."

"He wants my house."

"What?" Her eyes widened in surprise. "He made you take that house so he could keep the big one!"

"Shhh. Here they come."

"I'll just step into the kitchen and eavesdrop." Paula vanished into the back room.

"Lindsay, I'd like you to meet Rodney Bradford."

The tall man with gray hair, acne-scarred skin and dark eyes wore a business suit, but he didn't look like a business person...more like a member of the mob cleaned up for trial. He gave me a big smile and extended a large hand across the counter. "Good to meet you, Lindsay."

I took his hand automatically. It was thick, hard and callused. He didn't grip too tightly, didn't hang on too long, didn't do anything wrong, but something about him creeped me out. Maybe just because he was hanging with Rick. Or maybe it was something to do with the darkness that seemed to expand out from those eyes and surround the man.

Nah, that was silly. Probably just because he was hanging with Rick.

"Can we talk outside?" Bradford asked, his gaze shifting nervously around the restaurant, looking at the couple in the corner as if they might be spies.

"No," I said. "The acoustics are just fine in here. Feel free to speak."

"Lindsay." Rick spoke my name as if it was a threat, but then he gave a big salesman smile. "Please?"

I considered the situation. Stand there and argue with a man whose ears were tuned to hear only his own words or go outside with the two of them, then run back inside and lock the door. "Fine." I took a fortifying sip of my current Coke, set it on the counter and headed for the front door.

Outside I led them away from the door but still in the shade of my awning. It was a hot day. I stopped in front of the sign painted on my window, positioning myself directly beneath the words *Death by* and obscuring most of the word *Chocolate*. I figured that would make a nice picture, though Bradford was probably too dense to get it and Rick was too self-consumed.

"Rodney is interested in purchasing that little house you're living in, the one you and I own," Rick said, ramping up the wattage on his smile.

Jerk. Reminding me the house was still community property, that we were still legally—no, I can't say the "m" word when it relates to Rick. We were still legally bound.

I smiled with the same degree of sincerity as he did. That would be…none. "You mean my home? I'm not interested in selling."

"It would mean a whole lot to me," Rodney said. "My grandparents used to live there. That house has got sentimental value." He paused, blinked and seemed confused for a second. Was this guy sick? His tanned skin did look kind of pallid. He swallowed, recovered and continued. "I used to visit them when I was a boy. Some of the best memories of my life. Now they're—" He lowered his gaze, and this time his pause was deliberate. Con job. I'd seen Rick do it too many times not to recognize it. "They're in heaven, and I'd just like to be able to go to that old house, sleep in my old room, sit on the porch like we used to and remember the good times."

I was sorry to hear the nice elderly couple Rick and I bought the house from was dead. They'd seemed healthy, looking forward to life in a retirement village. "The house across the street is for sale. You could buy it, get a pair of binoculars and sit on the porch every day looking at my house."

"Lindsay!" Rick exclaimed.

Beads of sweat broke out on Rodney's forehead. The temperature was in the 80s, but the shade was cool. Was my refusal freaking him out that bad? "I've got a little money," he said. His voice suddenly sounded creaky. "I'll pay you more than you'd get anywhere else just so I can have my dear old grandmother's house."

"I'm sorry. It's not for sale. If you'll excuse me, I don't want to leave Paula with all the cleanup."

I took a step toward the door.

Rodney cleared his throat. "Could I have a glass of water?"

A stalling tactic. I sighed. "Sure."

I went inside.

Paula had come back from the kitchen to stand beside the door. "Don't sell him your house."

"Don't worry." I poured a glass of ice water and went back out, planning to hand it to the man then run inside while he was drinking.

He raised his head to look at me. His skin was really pale and his eyes had a shiny cast to them. Maybe this was more than frustration at being thwarted. My cookies had nuts. I hoped he wasn't allergic. If he went into anaphylactic shock and died, it wouldn't be good publicity for the diner.

He reached a hand toward the glass, his eyes rolled up in his head, he groaned and slowly crumpled to the sidewalk.

"Did you bring a drunk man into my restaurant?" I demanded of Rick, hoping that's what it was. I didn't need my place to be quarantined for an

7

outbreak of malaria or shut down because my cookies made somebody sick.

Rick sank to the ground beside the man. Paula rushed out. The couple at the corner table stood and looked through the window. I held onto the glass of water as if it was a glass of Coke and prayed for a verdict of too many beers.

"Call 911!" Rick shouted.

I set the water on the sidewalk, fumbled in the pocket of my jeans for my cell phone and punched in the three ominous numbers.

Paula rose, her face pale, her expression solemn. "Lindsay, he's dead."

The couple exploded through the door and hauled butt out of there. They didn't want to be seen on the ten o'clock news.

This was worse than getting sick. Heart attack? Nut allergies? Please, not poisoned chocolate again! "You don't know that he's dead," I snapped. "You thought your husband was dead just because you shot him, but he was still alive."

Rick stood. He'd lost his salesman's smile. Damn. That did not bode well.

Someone answered my phone call. "911. What is your emergency?"

I swallowed and spoke into the phone. "I think I just killed a man. I mean…my cookies killed a man. I mean—"

"He had the brownie," Paula interrupted.

I didn't correct the 911 lady. Cookies or brownies, a man had just died after eating my dessert.

Even if it was a good old-fashioned heart attack, death and desserts just don't go well together.

# Chapter Two

Within a matter of minutes an ambulance and two squad cars arrived with lights and sirens blaring.

I stood behind the counter gripping Paula's hand while the uniforms swarmed all over the sidewalk and into my restaurant. I wasn't holding her hand just to be supportive. She still had a problem dealing with cops even though her ex, a cop who'd abused her and tried to kill her, was safely behind prison bars. Mostly I was hanging onto her hand because I was afraid she would run away and hide, and that sort of action tends to look suspicious.

All things considered, she was doing pretty good, though she had a vise-like grip on my hand and was a few shades paler than normal.

"You the lady who called 911?" a big burly cop asked me.

"Yes." I cleared my throat. "Sir."

"You said you killed this man?"

"No! Well, yes, I probably said that, but I didn't mean *I* killed him."

The cop pushed his hat back on his head and scowled at me. Do they teach them Scowling 101 in the Police Academy? They all seemed to do it so well, and that included Adam Trent, the homicide

10

detective I was almost dating. "Then what did you mean?" he asked.

I threw one arm in the air, still restraining Paula with the other hand. "I don't know! I was upset! I just meant he died after eating dessert in my restaurant. I was worried he might have nut allergies. My cookies have nuts."

"Brownies," Paula interjected.

"My brownies have nuts too. There's a warning sign, but people don't always pay attention. I make nut-free brownies, but those don't sell as well, so I don't make them as often. Who wouldn't rather have nuts unless, of course, nuts make you sick." I was babbling. I could tell from the way the cop's eyes were starting to cross. "So, anyway, if I killed him, I didn't mean to." That still didn't sound right. "What did he die from?"

"We won't know until we get the autopsy results. What made you think he didn't die from natural causes?"

"I never said he didn't!"

The cop pulled out a small notepad and a pen. "I need your name, address and phone number."

Great. I wasn't anxious for this latest news to get back to Trent. We were already delayed in having any kind of a relationship because Rick wouldn't sign those freaking divorce papers, and now I was being questioned about a death right outside my restaurant. This latest incident wasn't likely to increase my aura of respectability.

I consoled myself with the thought that it could have been worse. At least I wouldn't have to deal with my parents for a couple of weeks. They were on a cruise to Alaska, enjoying cooler temperatures and, I hoped, out of cell phone and newscast range. They already considered me undependable and irresponsible. When they heard this latest news, it would somehow be my fault that the man died at my restaurant. If I'd been a little more responsible, he'd have died down the street outside the tattoo parlor.

I sighed and turned my attention to the cop. "My name is Lindsay Powell."

"It's Lindsay Kramer!" Rick shouted from a table across the room. Apparently his conversation with another cop wasn't enough to prevent his eavesdropping on my conversation.

I ignored him. "Lindsay Powell," I assured my cop. "I never changed my name. Women can do that now. That rude man who just shouted at me brought the dead man in here, and he was eating chocolate with him. He's the one you need to be questioning, not me."

"We're talking to everybody," my cop assured me. "Your address and phone number?"

\*\*\*

By the time Paula and I got rid of the cops and cleaned up the restaurant, it was late afternoon. Getting rid of the cops was the hardest part. Telling the 911 operator I had killed a man was not a good idea. I have often wished I had some kind of filter between my brain and my mouth. Unfortunately, they don't sell those on eBay.

Paula and I finished cleaning the restaurant, then I drove to my home that had, for a short while that day, doubled in value. With Rodney Bradford dead, my house had likely returned to its former minimal value.

Sure enough, it looked just the same as when I'd left it early that morning.

I stowed my elderly but still fast red Celica in my detached garage that lists to the southeast at about a twenty degree angle, walked out and tugged the creaky door closed behind me.

As I crossed my au naturel lawn, I reflected that it needed to be mowed. The dandelions were gaining on the clover. Not that it really bothered me. Dandelions have green leaves and pretty yellow flowers followed by fluffy white blossoms. Clover has pretty flowers and smells wonderful. Grass, on the other hand, does nothing but sit there and make demands...*water me, fertilize me, mow me, kill off my friends, the dandelions and clover*.

My house was small and old, the garage threatened to fall over every time the wind blew (and the wind blows a lot in Kansas City), and my lawn had more weeds than grass. Why was Bradford willing to pay so much money for this place?

Maybe his autopsy would reveal that he'd died from a brain tumor which had caused him to do inexplicable and irresponsible things like running naked down the middle of Interstate 435 in rush hour traffic, shouting bomb threats at the airport, and offering to buy rundown real estate for twice what it was worth.

As soon as I entered my front door, my cat, King Henry, strolled leisurely across the hardwood floor to greet me. He's a large animal, twenty-three pounds of solid muscle, white with gold markings on his face and tail. He moved in last fall and has been in control ever since.

He wound around my legs, purred and looked up at me with Frank Sinatra blue eyes. I leaned over and stroked his thick fur. "Glad to see me, big guy? I saved the homestead today. You could have been out on the streets again, homeless, like you were when you came here. Remember?"

He didn't. He gave a soft "rowr," turned and led me to the kitchen where he showed me his empty food bowl. That bowl got empty a lot. And we're not talking an ordinary kitty size dish. His head was too big to allow him to eat from one of those. I'd bought him a doggie bowl instead, and he did not like to see the bottom. I dutifully refilled it, and he dug in.

Music sounded in the distance. *Wild Bull Rider*. My ring tone for my other neighbor, Fred.

I pulled my not-all-that-smart phone from my purse.

"Why did you tell the police you killed a man?" Fred asked in greeting.

"How on earth do you know that?" Fred rarely left his house, kept the shades closed all the time, spent his days on the computer as a day trader (ha!) yet somehow always seemed to know more than the local psychic.

"If Rodney Bradford died from natural causes, you'll probably be okay, but it's not a good idea to bring yourself to the attention of local law enforcement when you drive as fast as you do."

"*If* he died of natural causes? Does this mean you don't know what killed Bradford? I'm astonished there's something you don't know!"

Henry went to the back door, stood on his hind legs and tried to turn the knob with his paws. Subtle, he's not. I opened the door to let him outside.

"I have no idea what caused Bradford's death," Fred said. "The police haven't finished the autopsy."

"So you get your information from the cops?" I asked, ever hopeful of tripping him up and learning something about him. It wouldn't surprise me if he got information from the police database. I knew for a fact that he sometimes hacked into computer systems where he shouldn't be hacking. Well, almost a fact. As close to as a fact as I was ever going to get with Fred.

Let's just say I had a strong suspicion he was a hacker.

He ignored my question. "I'm making *beef bourguignon*. Would you like to join me for dinner?"

"How do you know I haven't already eaten?"

"I don't know, but since you just arrived home, I assume you haven't had time to eat. Feeding that hair factory who lives with you would be your first priority."

Fred pretended he didn't like Henry and Henry pretended a supreme indifference to Fred. Actually, I don't think Henry was pretending.

Fred complained about Henry's shedding, and Henry tossed out a few extra hairs every time he got close to Fred.

15

"I'll bring dessert," I told Fred. I could almost hear him smiling. "Would you rather have chocolate cupcakes with cream cheese filling or chocolate fudge with peanut butter swirls?" I was teasing him. I knew the answer. "Or we could have both," I added.

"That'll be fine. Come over as soon as you get Henry back in the house." He hung up. Fred doesn't believe in protracted farewells.

There was no point in trying to figure out how he knew Henry was outside. I called my cat inside, grabbed the chocolate goodies I'd brought home from the shop, and headed next door.

Fred's house is older than mine, but you'd never know it. Everything down to the last splinter of wood and chip of paint is perfect. Last winter a piece of baseboard molding in his hallway separated from the wall by a fraction of an inch. I suggested he caulk it. I've caulked much wider gaps in my molding. Enough caulk can hide a multitude of sins. But Fred completely replaced the molding on both sides of his hallways so there'd be no gaps and both pieces would match perfectly.

Once I squashed a spider on his hardwood floor—but that's another story.

Needless to say, his yard is also perfect—every blade of grass exactly the same length, every leaf on every bush and tree symmetrical, all his flowers bright and in full bloom. Having my less-than-perfect yard next door has been good for him. It's taught him tolerance. Or maybe it's just taught him to look the other way when he leaves his house.

Fred answered my knock. "Bread just came out of the oven," he said and turned to head back to the kitchen.

Is there anything that smells better than freshly-baked bread? Okay, maybe my freshly baked chocolate chip cookies, but bread's a close second.

I followed the aroma and Fred's tall, lanky frame through his shadowed living room to his kitchen with its wall of windows looking out on a forest of trees in his back yard. Those are the only windows in his house not covered by blinds. Of course, the trees create an effective curtain of greenery. Fred does not suffer from claustrophobia.

He busied himself at his stove, and I sat down at his shiny oak table that, like the wire-framed glasses he wears, never gets smudged. With his white hair—always immaculate, of course—I'd guess Fred's age to be somewhere between forty and sixty. It's hard to be more exact, and he's not going to tell.

He served the beef concoction with a side of fresh asparagus, home-made bread with real butter and wine from a bottle with a cork in it. Fred never does anything by half.

I took a bite of the beef. "This is wonderful." Fortunately Fred's culinary expertise doesn't extend to chocolate. If it did, I'd have to kill him. There's only room for one chocolatier in this town.

"Thank you," Fred replied as he meticulously transferred every mushroom from his plate to mine.

"Not that I'm complaining about getting extra mushrooms, but why do you use them if you don't like them?"

Fred looked at me as if I'd just asked why the sun always rose in the east. "I put them in because the recipe calls for them. I take them out because I don't like them."

It had been a stupid question.

"That guy who got killed, Rodney Bradford, he wanted to buy my house for a lot more money than it's worth."

"Uh huh."

"How did you know that?"

Fred paused in the process of slathering butter on his bread. "You just told me."

"Oh. Well, why do you think he made that offer?"

Fred ate a bite of beef, a bite of bread and a bite of asparagus. "I have no idea," he finally said. "Do you?"

I sipped the rich red wine from a cut-crystal glass and shook my head. "Not really. Rick said the man's grandparents used to live here, and he wanted the place for sentimental reasons. You knew the previous owners, didn't you?"

"I moved in here a year before they left. You know a year isn't time enough for me to develop a social relationship."

I smiled. "Except with me."

"You're difficult to avoid. Besides, those people never offered me chocolate."

"Nevertheless, I know how nosy you are. You're bound to have noticed something. Did you ever meet their grandson?"

I waited while he ate another sequence of beef, bread and asparagus. "I believe I do remember a younger man coming to stay for a few weeks about five years ago. It could have been a grandson."

"Five years and how many months?"

Fred paused in his eating and looked thoughtful.

"I'm kidding! I don't really need to know how many months. I was just—never mind. What did the guy look like?"

Fred shrugged. "I don't recall a lot about him. Medium height, thin brown hair."

The man could have gained weight, his hair could have gone gray and Fred, who stood well over six feet, probably had a different definition of *medium height* than I did. "Do you remember his name?"

"I don't believe we were ever introduced."

"I suppose it could be the same guy. Maybe he really did want my house for sentimental reasons. But even if that part's true, I'd be willing to bet that Rick was up to something."

"Or Bradford was up to something. He just got out of prison."

"What?" I almost choked on a piece of potato from the beef concoction.

"I said, he just got out of prison." Fred can be annoyingly literal.

"When?"

"Two months ago." He calmly cut another slice of bread, the mundane act at odds with the information he'd just imparted.

"What was he in prison for?"

"Committing a crime."

Not that literal. He was jacking with me. He does that a lot. "Any crime in particular?"

"Of course. They don't send people to prison for nonspecific crimes." He ate a few more bites, making me wait. I poked him with my fork.

"Patience, Lindsay," he said. "You need to learn patience. Bradford served three years for burglary. Homeowner woke up in the middle of the night to go to the bathroom and caught Bradford heading out the door with the silverware. It was a house in Prairie Village over on the Kansas side. The silverware was the real thing. The homeowner chased him outside and got his license plate. The police found other stolen items in Bradford's home, and the man went to prison."

"I thought he looked like a criminal! Well, I thought he looked like a mobster. I guess I was giving him too much credit. So he was just a petty burglar." I sipped my wine and contemplated the fact that Rick was involved with a convicted felon. Could I somehow use that knowledge against him, force him to sign the divorce papers by threatening to expose his friendship with a criminal?

Probably not. Who'd care? He was already involved in half the shady real estate deals in the Kansas City area. One more criminal associate wouldn't make a noticeable difference.

Fred chewed, swallowed and took a sip of wine. "It does give rise to the question of why a petty burglar wanted your house so badly."

That was a very good question. "Maybe he needed a place close to your house so he could know when you were gone, break in here and steal your old movies." Fred had one entire room dedicated to movies, especially old movies. They're organized by VCR tape vs. DVD, then, within those physical categories, all are in order by title and cross-referenced on a dedicated computer by actors and subjects. Did I mention he's a little OCD?

"Maybe," he said.

"Or maybe he planned to break into your house and hack into your computer and find out just what it is you do all day." I was being sort of facetious, but not totally. It was possible that Rick's felonious client wanted access to Fred's house and Fred's secrets. Those secrets could be valuable. That seemed much more likely than his wanting my house because his dear old grandmother once lived there.

Fred ate his last bite of beef and drank his last sip of wine. Of course they ended at the same time. "I doubt Bradford would be smart enough to do that."

"He could be just a front man for somebody bigger, somebody who is smart enough." Another thought occurred to me. "And rich enough. If Bradford was stealing silverware for a living, where did he get the money to make such an outrageous offer on my house?"

Fred set his glass on the table and nodded. "Valid point. Maybe the reason he wanted your house has something to do with the reason he was killed."

"He was killed? When I talked to you a few minutes ago, you said you didn't know how he died! Do you know something I don't know?"

"I know lots of things you don't know. Did you bring the chocolate?"

He knew I brought the chocolate. The plastic containers were sitting on his counter. He was trying to change the subject.

Rodney Bradford's autopsy might not be complete yet. The cops might not know the cause of Bradford's death, but I had a sick feeling we'd all soon hear that the man had been murdered.

# Chapter Three

I turned down Fred's invitation to watch an old movie after dinner. I wouldn't have minded another viewing of *The Day the Earth Stood Still* (the original, no remakes for Fred), but I wanted to have time to talk to Paula before we both had to call it a night in order to get up at 4:00 a.m.

Paula's house was on the other side of mine. In the gathering dusk, I crossed Fred's golf-green yard, my easy-care yard and Paula's normal yard. When I reached her front porch, I was surprised to see the interior door open, only the screen closed. That was a good sign compared to the days when she had all the doors and windows triple-locked in a futile attempt to stay safe from her crazy ex-husband.

"Anlinny!" Zach spotted me and charged to the door, pressing his small hands, nose and forehead to the screen and looking really strange. *Anlinny* is his way of saying *Aunt Lindsay*. He was a big boy of two and a half and spoke most words semi-coherently, but I fear I will still be *Anlinny* when he graduates from college.

I grinned down at him. "Hi, Hot Shot."

"Lindsay," Paula said, pulling Zach aside and opening the door. "Come on in."

"Got cookies?" Zach asked hopefully.

"No," Paula said firmly. "You've had enough sugar for one day. You can visit with Aunt Lindsay for fifteen minutes, then you're going to bed."

Zach opened his arms, and I reached down and scooped him up for a big hug. He was a happy kid with his mother's blonde hair, blue eyes and sweet disposition and, thank goodness, none of his father's evil traits.

I carried him over to the beige sofa and sat down with him in my lap.

Paula's house is the same era as Fred's and mine. Pretty much the whole neighborhood is except for that one place up the street that burned down in the '50s and got replaced by a really ugly square building.

Inside, however, our homes are very different. My house is furnished with bright colors and mismatched odds and ends I found at antique stores and garage sales. Fred's is solidly masculine and sedately tasteful without a piece of lint or dust. Paula's house, in spite of her attempts to create a bland setting with nondescript furnishings, is a riotous place of toys and games. In her attempts to hide from the world, Paula tried to make her person and her home invisible. However, Zach took care of adding a touch of individuality with his colorful toys. I bought him several of those toys like the bright red fire engine, the bright orange truck, the bright green ball…you get the idea.

Zach tolerated my hugging on him for about thirty seconds then slid down and charged across the room. That kid has only two speeds—damn the torpedoes or sound asleep.

"I'm glad you came by." Paula moved a coloring book off the sofa and took a seat beside me. "That man dropping…" she glanced in Zach's direction "…dropping to the sidewalk in front of the restaurant was disturbing."

"Disturbing? Yeah, you could say that, but only if you wanted to make a gross understatement."

Zach trotted over clutching the green ball that was almost as big as he was. "Play!" He handed me the ball then ran across the room and plopped down facing me.

I moved to the floor and rolled the ball to him. He laughed in delight and rolled it back to me. Men are so easy to entertain at that age. Come to think of it, give them a ball at any age and they're happy. Football, golf ball, baseball…men are fascinated with their balls.

"How about a glass of wine?" Paula offered.

I'd already had a glass at Fred's, but it wasn't like I'd have to drive home. I could easily crawl over to my house if the need arose. I rolled the ball to Zach again. "Sure, and pour an extra big one for yourself."

"Oh?" Paula gave me a questioning glance then disappeared into the kitchen.

"Have you been a good boy?" I asked Zach.

He clutched his ball, shook his head and giggled. "No!"

"That's my boy," I encouraged.

"Can I have Coke?" he asked hopefully.

I glanced up to see Paula returning from the kitchen with two glasses of white wine and a red sippy cup. The red sippy cup was a gift from me since Zach always wanted to drink from my red can.

"Of course," I said even though I knew the cup probably contained juice or milk.

Paula gave Zach his cup and sat on the sofa, handing me a glass of wine then drinking delicately from the other. Paula's petite, blonde and tiny, and most of her movements are fluid and delicate. I'm tall and gangly with freckles and messy red hair and have been known to trip over the grain in my hardwood floors. I'd hate her, but she's so nice, that's just not possible.

I resumed my seat on the sofa and lifted my glass to Zach in a toast. He raised his sippy cup, and we both said, "Cheers!" then drank.

"Bottoms up," Paula advised her son. "It's your bedtime. You want to get to sleep in time to see all your dreams."

"No!" Zach dropped his sippy cup to the floor and charged across the room to me. "I want to stay with Anlinny!" He grabbed my knees and looked up, his expression that of a man about to be hanged. "I stay with you!"

I leaned over and pulled him into my lap. "How about I take you upstairs and tuck you into bed?" I smoothed his soft hair and kissed the top of his head.

"No!"

Over the last couple of months, that had become his favorite word.

Paula rose. "Yes. Say good night to Aunt Lindsay."

"No!"

Eventually the two of us got him upstairs and into bed. I think he was asleep before his head hit his Lion King pillowcase.

Paula left the door slightly ajar, and we returned to the living room.

"All right," Paula said, resuming her seat on the sofa, "we have alcohol, and I brought home a couple of leftover cookies if we need them. I think we're ready to talk about the possible side effects of a dead body in front of our restaurant."

I sat next to her and took another drink of wine. If I hadn't already eaten two cupcakes and one piece of fudge, I'd have asked her to bring on the cookies. I do love chocolate. "Fred says that man just got out of prison."

Paula's eyes widened. "The dead man?"

"Yes. The terminally ill man Rick brought into our restaurant to try to talk me into selling my house."

Paula frowned and set her glass on her nondescript coffee table beside a pile of colorful plastic blocks. "The man was terminally ill? What was wrong with him?"

"I don't know, but he died. That sounds pretty terminal to me."

"So you don't know what caused his death?"

"Not yet. But I do know he got out of prison two months ago." I repeated the story Fred had told me.

27

Paula gave a huge sigh and shook her head. "This gets worse all the time. An ex-con drops dead outside a place where people come to relax and eat."

"Drops dead after a failed attempt to talk me into selling my house to him."

"Do you think Rick knew about his client's past?"

I thought about that for a moment. "It's possible he didn't know, but real estate agents do quite a bit of pre-qualifying before they spend any time working with a client. However, if Rick smelled money, he wouldn't care if the guy was a mass murderer and escaped from prison the day before, killing two guards and seven inmates in the process. If he stood to get a big fee out of the deal, Rick wouldn't give it a second thought before moving Ted Bundy in next door to any of us."

"Well, I guess it doesn't matter since the guy's dead." She picked up her glass and drained the contents.

"Yeah, and maybe nobody but us and that one couple saw it and it won't affect our business."

Paula nodded. "Everything will be back to normal tomorrow."

I shuddered. Normal except for the memory of watching a man die in front of me. "I may have a hard time walking over that part of the sidewalk tomorrow," I said.

"You'll get over it. I shot my ex and thought he died. After that, I'm not squeamish about seeing somebody die from a problem I didn't cause. In a couple of days, you'll be fine." She gave me a reassuring smile. For all her fragile appearance, Paula is one tough lady.

"If it ever gets to the point I have to shoot Rick, I'm calling you to help me hide the body."

"No problem."

I believed her.

I went home and climbed the stairs to bed. Henry followed close on my heels.

For the most part, Henry is an ideal sleeping partner. He stays at the foot of the bed, snores very softly and doesn't hog the covers. When he first came to live with me, he had occasional moments of gratitude for a roof over his head and a full food bowl. I'd wake to the feel of a furry face rubbing on my cheek and the sound of purring that was so loud I'm surprised Fred didn't hear it and complain. I'd pet him, say "You're welcome," and he'd go back to the foot of the bed. After a couple of months, however, he came to take his new home for granted, and the middle-of-the-night outbursts of gratitude stopped.

But that night I woke to the sound of what I thought was loud purring. Still half-asleep, I reached to pet him and mumbled, "You're welcome."

He wasn't purring. He was growling deep in his throat. That was not a good sign.

Henry nudged my forehead, growled again then leapt to the floor.

The last time he went through this freak-out routine was a few months ago when Paula's husband broke into my house and poisoned my chocolate pudding cake.

I sat up in bed, suddenly wide awake, heart pounding, adrenalin pumping as I surged into fight or flight mode. The numbers on the digital clock glowed brightly—1:30 a.m. "Henry," I said softly, hopefully, "did you have a bad dream? Why don't you come back to bed and we'll cuddle?"

In the moonlight I could see his white form as he stretched up to bat at the knob of my closed bedroom door. He was not coming back to bed until he had a chance to check out whatever had disturbed him. A bad dream? A panic attack? Perhaps the sound of another cat outside, invading his territory? That was surely all it was. No big deal. No reason for me to get upset.

I was unable to reassure myself.

I got out of bed and went over to Henry. "Need a midnight snack?" I asked. "I get a little grumpy when my blood sugar gets low, too."

He opened his large mouth, bared his half-inch fangs and let loose with a yowl that would have done his ancestors in the jungle proud. That should, I thought, scare off any usurpers of his territory. It certainly made my hair stand on end.

I opened the door, and Henry streaked across the hall then flowed down the stairs. I followed, though with much less haste and grace. I wasn't all that eager to confront whatever Henry thought was downstairs.

My brain told me there could be nothing threatening in my house. The doors were locked securely. My only emotion should be annoyance at my cat for waking me in the middle of the night. But my gut had a completely different attitude. It conjured images of murderous lunatics, hideous monsters and bloodthirsty ghouls. Seeing a man die in front of me had probably given my imagination a huge boost.

Henry trotted quietly but determinedly through the living room and into the kitchen.

*Please let him be hungry.*

By the time I caught up with him, he was standing at the door to the basement, peering intently as if he could see through the wood.

A lot of people in the Kansas City area finish out their basements and put rec rooms or guest suites down there. Shoot a little pool while waiting out a tornado, stick your visiting relatives below ground so you can't hear them yell at each other. Some people have windows and even a door in their basement.

Mine is old, built at a time when people used basements to shelter from tornadoes and store home-canned veggies, not to entertain. It has stone walls, a brick floor and lots of spiders. Maybe a ghost or two. I rarely go down there during the day. I had no intention of going in the middle of the night.

Henry did his stand-up-and-paw-the-knob routine then sat back and looked at me, waiting.

A thousand scenes raced through my head, all ending in my bloody demise. I tried to listen to see if I could hear any sounds from the basement. If my heart would just quit pounding so loudly, I might have been able to hear something or at least verify that there was nothing to be heard.

Henry's ears pricked. He stood, back arched, tail curling high into the air, and scratched at the door.

My mouth went dry.

A mouse, I told myself. There was probably a mouse down there. Henry sometimes brought me a mouse for a gift. I always took it from him and disposed of it, though I told him I ate it and it was quite delicious. That's what was happening here. A mouse in the basement had his attention, and he was determined to catch it for my breakfast.

Then I heard it. A scraping sound. Muffled by the closed door, but definitely a scraping sound.

Did mice scrape? They have claws, so it was possible.

I raced through the house, checking the front and back doors and all the windows. Everything was securely locked. Since the basement had no outside door, there could not be anyone down there...unless it was somebody who could walk through walls.

Not likely.

I picked up my marble rolling pin from my kitchen counter then returned to the basement door. Henry stretched upward and tried in vain to get that door open. He turned and glared at me, then went back to his efforts. That door has one of the original cut glass knobs, and Henry actually seemed to get some traction on the bevels of that knob. It turned a fraction of an inch.

I slammed my body against the door and pushed Henry away.

He gave me a disdainful look that clearly accused me of being a coward.

I groaned. There was no help for it. I had to go downstairs. I wouldn't be able to sleep again until I made sure there was no boogey man in my basement. Besides, I couldn't let my cat think I was a coward.

Against my better judgment, I fetched the flip flops I kept beside the kitchen door so the bricks of the basement floor wouldn't rip up my feet. I saw no point in finding a robe to wear over my tee-shirt. I was preparing to descend into a dark dungeon to confront a demon. Modesty was the least of my concerns.

I retrieved a flashlight from below the sink and tucked it under one arm, tightened my grip on my rolling pin, drew in a deep breath and took hold of that glass knob. I turned to look at Henry, hoping to find him yawning, bored with this game, ready to go back to bed. He stood on full alert, gaze fixed on the basement door.

Damn.

Like pulling a Band-aid off quickly to shorten the pain, I turned the knob, jerked the door open and braced myself for an attack.

Nothing but a hint of damp, musty air.

Nothing to be afraid of. But that didn't stop the perspiration from popping out on my upper lip.

I flipped a switch just inside the door, and a bulb hanging from the ceiling at the bottom of the stairs flared, spreading light over the wooden steps and a portion of bare brick floor. Granted, that was only a small portion of the basement, but it was enough to satisfy me.

"Happy now?" I asked, hoping this view of emptiness would also satisfy my attack-cat.

He gave me one brief glance then streaked past me, down the steps, across the lighted area and into the darkness.

Double damn.

What if there really was somebody in the basement, somebody who could hurt Henry?

With long, sharp claws and teeth which he used at lightning speed, Henry was not defenseless.

But what if that mysterious person in the basement had a gun and shot my cat?

Oh, good grief. I was really letting my imagination run wild. There was no person in the basement. No monster, no ghoul. Just a mouse. Maybe a squirrel or chipmunk.

With flashlight in my left hand, rolling pin in my right and heart pounding loudly in my ears, I started down the stairs. One step at a time, I descended deeper and deeper into that spooky basement.

Spider webs decorated the corners of the lighted area. Shivers of movement indicated some of the spiders were at home and startled by my invasion. I'd cleaned the entire basement when I moved in a year before but hadn't given much thought to it after that. Like the dandelions in my yard, the spiders were free to come and go so long as they stayed in their own domain.

Five doors opened off the main area. One was an old utility room, one held racks for wine, one was lined with shelves for canned goods, one was completely empty, and the last was an old furnace room that dated from the days when coal was the primary fuel source.

"Henry!" I whispered.

I aimed my flashlight into the utility room. A white, translucent form floated into the glare. I gasped, jumped backward and nearly dropped my light.

Another freaking spider web. I'd almost had a heart attack over a spider web.

I forced myself to walk past that web to the center of the small room and pull the chain to turn on the light. Nothing anywhere but dust.

I stepped back into the central area and called again, louder this time. It was my house. I didn't have to whisper. "Henry! Get out here! Now!" My voice bounced back to me from the stone walls. I should have stuck to whispering.

Sometimes Henry comes when I call, like when I'm holding a can of tuna or some fresh catnip. Other times he seems to be deaf. They do not make cat hearing aids, though this appears to be a common problem with cats.

A low hiss drew me to the furnace room. I stepped to the entrance and directed the beam of my flashlight into the room. The blackness of the walls, stained from years of coal dust, swallowed my puny light.

Like a ghost-cat, Henry stood, back arched, tail erect, poised in battle-ready stance, glaring at the outside wall with its boarded-up coal chute. He'd probably chased a mouse who squirmed through the cracks and escaped. Nevertheless, his staring at the wall was spooky and did absolutely nothing to ease my sense of dread.

"Okay, buddy, no more catnip for you if you're going to hallucinate."

Abruptly he relaxed, turned and walked past me, rubbing against my leg and spreading coal dust as he went. Whatever had been upsetting him was gone, and he wasn't one to dwell on the past.

"Henry! Come back here! Do *not* get in my bed!" I dashed upstairs after him.

He demanded to go outside, and I was happy to let him.

While he was...I hoped...taking a bath, I retrieved the basement door skeleton key from the top of the refrigerator. *Skeleton key.* The name itself gave me a creepy feeling under the present circumstances.

I closed the basement door securely, locked it and left the key in the keyhole. I saw an old movie at Fred's house where they did that so the door couldn't be unlocked from the other side. Of course, I saw another old movie where the person trapped in the room slid a newspaper under the door then poked the key out and retrieved it by pulling the newspaper holding the key inside. Not that a mouse was likely to bring a newspaper with him so I felt safe leaving the key in the door.

Henry's face appeared at the screen door, and I let him in. He looked cleaner so I allowed him to join me in bed, though I did drape an old towel over his area just in case he was still hiding some of that coal dust in his thick fur.

Adrenalin does not leave as rapidly as it comes, and for the rest of the night I dozed in and out of sleep and was actually grateful when the alarm went off at 4:00 so I could stop trying so hard to sleep.

We went downstairs, and Henry trotted over to that blasted basement door again but gave it a quick sniff and continued on to his food bowl.

Must have been a mouse. Maybe I should think about getting an exterminator.

# Chapter Four

In spite of Paula's and my concerns about the dead man having an impact on business, Tuesday got off to a really good start. Nobody asked suspicious questions or carefully stepped around the part of the sidewalk where Bradford did the dead thing.

Our usual breakfast crowd, most still half-asleep, scarfed down rolls and pastries and drank gallons of Paula's coffee and my tea. I don't drink coffee and have been informed that my efforts to brew it rank right up there with swamp water that's past its expiration date. Since coffee always tastes that way to me, I can't judge, but I'm happy to let Paula take on that responsibility. I brew quite nice tea and open cans of Coke with panache. One cannot expect to be an expert at everything.

Around 9:00 we put up the *Closed* sign and began preparing for lunch. The special for the day would be Chicken Salad Sandwich with Chocolate Marble Cheesecake. We always have chocolate chip cookies, of course. Some people can't get through the day without a couple. I'm one of those people.

As I worked on the cookies, something I've done so many times it doesn't require a lot of attention, I told Paula about Henry's episode in the middle of the night. Made a joke of it. Laughed about my big, macho cat charging down to the basement and being given the slip by a mouse covered in coal dust.

Paula didn't laugh. "This is an odd time of year for mice to be getting into your house. They usually try to get inside during the fall when cold weather's coming on, not in summer."

I shrugged and added a few more chocolate chips to my cookie mixture. You can't have too many chocolate chips. "I'll go downstairs and have a closer look when I get home." *When it's daylight.*

Paula chopped chicken for her sandwiches. "Might be a raccoon or possum or some other kind of creature. These old houses have cracks you don't always know about."

Somehow the idea of cracks in my basement large enough to allow a raccoon or possum to come inside didn't make me feel even a little bit better.

The phone rang, interrupting our conversation about nighttime visitors.

"Lindsay, it's Adam Trent." *Detective* Adam Trent. Could be *My Boyfriend* Adam Trent if Rick would sign those blasted divorce papers. I call him *Trent*, so when he used his full name, a chill darted down my spine. This must be business, and the only business I could think of was the guy who dropped dead outside my restaurant yesterday. I recalled Fred's comment from last night, *Maybe the reason he wanted your house has something to do with the reason he was killed.*

"Hello, Adam Trent. Can I interest you in a cookie?"

He ignored my suggestive comment. "I need you to come down to the station to give a statement about Rodney Bradford's death." He paused. "You could bring some cookies when you come." The man has a chocolate tooth, especially where my desserts are concerned.

"I gave a statement to the cop who was here yesterday. I have nothing else to state."

Trent let out a long slow sigh. "That was when we thought his death might be from natural causes, before we got the results of the autopsy."

"And?" I prompted. He likes to do that cop thing of keeping everything a big secret. "It wasn't natural causes?"

"No."

"So it wasn't from natural causes, and I'm pretty sure the guy wasn't shot, stabbed or hanged." I was getting a really bad feeling. There weren't a lot of murder options left. "You can tell me. I won't tell anybody."

He hesitated. He really likes to keep his cop stuff a big secret.

"It's going to be all over the news tonight. You might as well tell me."

"Bradford was poisoned."

That cold chill returned and brought some buddies with it. "Poisoned? What kind of poison? Please tell me he wasn't allergic to nuts or chocolate or—"

Paula came up beside me, a questioning look on her face.

"No. Calm down," Trent said. "He was poisoned with amoprine berries. It's a plant in the deadly nightshade family."

I quickly ran through everything we'd served in the restaurant yesterday. No berries. I had raspberries for the cheesecake today, but they'd arrived only a few hours ago. Whew! I was off the hook. I looked at Paula and shook my head.

"I don't serve those," I told Trent. "That's my statement."

Trent sighed again. "Of course you don't. Nobody's suggesting you poisoned him. It's a slow-acting toxin. He had to consume it at least a couple of hours before he got to your place. You're not under suspicion, but we still need you to come in. You were talking to him when he died."

"So was Rick."

Long pause. "We're bringing Rick in too."

That wasn't good. Rick hated Trent. Although Rick kicked me out so he could move his girlfriend of the month into our house, he blamed Trent for the breakup of our marriage. That's Rick. Rewrites history until he gets it just the way he wants it.

"Are *you* going to question him?" I asked.

"No. Lawson will have that honor."

"That's good. I'd hate for you to have to kill him."

"Really?"

"Only because you might get in trouble for it. All right, what time do you want me there to describe in graphic detail the act of a man dropping to the sidewalk in front of me? Can it wait until we close this afternoon?"

"Sure. How about around five? We could go get an early dinner afterward."

"Sounds good." I'd have liked to invite him to my house for dessert afterward, but that wasn't going to happen until my divorce from Rick the Dick was final.

"Five o'clock then. Don't forget the cookies."

I hung up and turned to Paula, relating the details of my conversation with Trent. "Bradford was murdered. An ex-con was poisoned right here in front of our restaurant, and it's probably going to be on the ten o'clock news! I can just hear it. *Murder victim dies from poisoning at Death by Chocolate.* I don't think that's going to help our business. Damn Rick for bringing that man in here! Rick's the gift that keeps on giving, kind of like a venereal disease."

Paula laughed. "He should come with a warning sign."

I slid a pan of cookies into the oven and set the timer for eight minutes. "Maybe they'll arrest Rick for Bradford's murder."

"Not if the poison took two hours to work. He was only here with the guy for about an hour."

"I forgot about that. Bummer."

\*\*\*

Between finishing up at the restaurant and meeting with the cops I had time to go home and check on King Henry. He met me at the door, wound around my legs, purred and did his suck-up routine, then led me to his food bowl.

I dumped in more nuggets and left him eating contentedly while I took the flashlight and went to the basement. I paused at the top of the steps and looked back at him to see how he'd react to my venture, if he'd show any concern that I was going downstairs where the monster lived. Nothing on his mind but food.

I headed straight for the furnace room, went inside and pulled the chain in the center of the room to turn on the light.

Yuck!

Coal dust was everywhere, but not in a smooth layer as if it had settled there over the past year of my neglect. Certainly Henry accounted for some of the disturbance, but not all of it. Another critter had definitely been there. A whole herd of critters, judging from the mess.

Walking through that mess and probably ruining my favorite pair of sneakers, I moved over to the boarded up coal chute. I had no idea how many years the boards had been there. The black dust had probably permeated to their centers.

I held the light close and examined the cracks between the thick boards. The wood had warped very little over the years, and the largest space was about a quarter inch. Mice seemed to be able to slide through holes much smaller than their bodies, so perhaps this was where our nighttime intruder entered. If so, it couldn't be anything bigger than a mouse.

I grasped the structure and tried to shake it. It held firm.

I was being paranoid, getting all freaked out about a little mouse. A very little mouse, judging from the size of the crack.

Nevertheless, I made a cursory examination of the blackened stone walls and found no more open spaces. The red brick floor looked as though it had been through an earthquake, but that was to be expected with the shifting of the black clay soil in the area. The floor had been laid directly on the dirt with no mortar between the bricks. Probably a snug fit when it was done a hundred years ago.

A few bricks in the far corner of the room appeared to be even more disturbed, as if they'd lifted from their places then been pushed down again. I leaned over and studied the area carefully. Some of the black stuff appeared to be dirt rather than coal dust. Did mice dig? They had claws, so I supposed they could, and so could Henry. I'd seen the damage he could do to a tree trunk when he sharpened his claws. It was possible he'd dug up some dirt from between the bricks in an effort to reach whatever creature was in there last night.

I straightened and looked around. It was a creepy room, a filthy room, and there were probably lots of mice who came in to keep the spiders company.

I looked around at the spider webs. The only ones in this room were up high in the corners. Nothing at person-height. That was odd.

Something brushed against my leg. I screamed. My flashlight crashed to the floor and winked out. I ran toward the open door, taking advantage of the flight rather than the fight option.

A distinctive meow stopped me. I turned back to see Henry examining the dead flashlight.

I clutched my chest. "Henry! What are you doing down here? You almost caused me to have a heart attack!"

He regarded me serenely.

I went over, jerked the chain to turn off the light, snatched up the flashlight and my cat and stalked back upstairs.

Along with an exterminator, I needed a more sensitive cat.

\*\*\*

I only had to wait about five minutes at the police station before Trent came out to get me. He had a file folder in his hand and a scowl on his chiseled face. The scowl didn't necessarily mean anything bad. He just had to keep up with the other cops, show he didn't flunk Scowling 101.

I smiled at him. "In that suit and tie, you look official, almost like a cop."

He gave me a quick, unofficial grin. "In those tight jeans and that red blouse, you look like a woman who's got a hot date."

I turned to give him a glimpse of the rhinestones on my back pockets. I was dressed in my best. I'd even put on a clean pair of sneakers.

"How am I supposed to conduct an official interview when my mind is going to be on your sparkly butt?" he whispered.

I smiled, shrugged and tried to look innocent.

Trent reached for me, and for a moment I thought he was going to give me a hug right there in the police station.

Instead he lifted a white hair off my shirt.

"Henry likes to mark me before I leave home," I said. "Doesn't want me taking up with any other cats."

Trent rolled his eyes and motioned with the folder that I should go down the hall.

The room to which he directed me was small and grim and held only a scarred wooden table and uncomfortable wooden chairs. I sat in one. Trent took the seat across from me and laid the folder between us.

I looked up at the wall opposite me. "One way mirror?"

He nodded.

I grinned. "Kinky."

He has great eyes, brown with hints of green like the trees in early spring. Those eyes widened and became brighter with more green. He blushed and lowered his gaze to the table but not before I saw a trace of a smile.

The door opened, and a tall, thin man with immaculate iron gray hair, a perfectly fitted suit and a stern expression entered. Gerald Lawson. He and Trent worked together often, and he was a devout fan of my chocolate.

"Detective Lawson," I greeted. "I'm delighted you could join us. I hear you've been talking to my evil ex. Did you lock him up?"

He slid onto the chair next to the door and ignored my attempt to get information out of him. "Trent said you were bringing cookies."

I shook my head and sighed. "You men. All you want from a girl is chocolate chip cookies."

Without any change in expression, Lawson nodded. "With nuts."

"With nuts," I affirmed and lifted a canvas bag onto the table.

I'm working on converting the entire police force from donuts to cookies. It may not be any healthier for them, but it will be better for my business.

"Tell me about the incident in front of your restaurant yesterday," Lawson requested.

"You mean the incident where a man dropped dead in front of me?"

Lawson didn't blink. "That would be the incident." One of these days, I'm going to break him.

I lifted my hands, palms upward. "We were talking, and he dropped dead. That's all I can tell you."

"What were you talking about?"

"My house. He wanted to buy my house. My ex is a real estate agent, and he brought this Bradford guy in to try to talk me into selling."

"Your ex is in commercial real estate. Your house is not commercial property. Why was he working this deal?"

"You'll have to ask him." I was pretty sure he already had.

"So you told Mr. Bradford that you didn't want to sell your house?"

I shrugged. "I had no idea he'd take rejection so badly."

I thought I saw a hint of a smile, but that could have been wishful thinking on my part. "He offered you twice what your house is worth?"

"If you already know all this, why are you asking me?"

"It's called taking a statement. We don't know your side of the story officially until you tell us."

"*My* side of the story?" I leaned across the table. "*My* side is the *only* side! What's Rick been telling you? He brought that ex-con into my restaurant, and the man tried to buy my house for twice what it's worth. When I refused, he dropped dead. That's the whole story."

Trent and Lawson exchanged glances.

"How do you know he's an ex-con?" Lawson asked quietly.

I had no idea what illegal database Fred had hacked into in order to obtain that information. I valued that trait in him, would probably need it in the future, so I wasn't about to sell him out. "Oh, for goodness sake, you can find anything on the internet." That was a true statement.

"Some people can find anything on the internet," Trent said. "You have trouble finding your own Facebook page."

"I may have trouble, but that doesn't mean I can't do it. What difference does it make where I found out about Bradford's prison history?"

Trent folded his hands on the table. "Everything matters when we're investigating a murder."

I couldn't see myself all that well in the kinky mirror, but I'm pretty sure I went pale around my freckles. "You're not investigating *me*, are you? I never met that man before yesterday!"

"You told the 911 operator that you thought you killed him."

I threw my hands into the air. "Oh, for crying out loud! Does everybody in the county know about that stupid phone call? I was freaked out! I thought maybe he was allergic to nuts!"

Trent nodded. He knew me, knew I wasn't guilty, but the look on his face made me question my own innocence. I could see him getting a perp to confess just by giving him that look.

"Why do you think he wanted your house so badly that he got your ex to act as his agent and offered you twice what it's worth?" Lawson asked.

"I have no idea." I didn't volunteer my theory that it was to get close to Fred.

We went through the entire incident in graphic, boring detail again, "for the record." I'd been looking forward to the chance to be with Trent, but this was not my idea of a fun date. Maybe next time we could schedule a visit to the dentist for matching root canals.

Finally with all the questions answered at least twice, it seemed to be over.

Lawson and Trent exchanged glances again, and Lawson gave a small, almost imperceptible nod.

Trent shifted a little in his chair and met my gaze full on. Did I mention he has gorgeous eyes? I could get lost in those eyes. "Lindsay, one more thing."

"Yes?"

"About Rick." He sounded tentative. Adam Trent never sounds tentative.

"Yes?"

"Did you know he was seeing Bradford's wife?"

"What?!" I shot to my feet. I don't know why it surprised me that Rick was dating a married woman. It had never bothered him to date other women while we were married. But dating a woman who was married to his ex-convict client seemed to take the whole cheating thing to new heights.

"I take that as a *no.*"

I sighed and sat back down, fervently wishing I'd never heard of Rick Kramer. Don't ask me to explain why I ever married such a creep in the first place. It seemed like a good idea at the time. Of course, dying my hair bright blue the day before my senior prom also seemed like a good idea at the time.

"Yes," I said, "that's a *no.* I don't keep up with Rick's women. Does this make Rick a suspect?"

"All I can say is that Rick's a person of interest."

"He's really not, you know."

Trent arched a dubious eyebrow. "You believe he's innocent?"

"Of the murder? Oh, probably. He might kill for money or power but not for a woman. He's not capable of that kind of passion for a woman. But that's not what I'm saying. I'm just saying he's not a person of interest. He's actually pretty boring when you get to know him."

Trent almost laughed. The lines at the corners of his eyes lifted. Lawson remained impassive, of course.

"Can I still get a divorce if Rick goes to prison?"

Trent shrugged. "Yeah. Probably make it easier."

At least the interview ended on a positive note.

# Chapter Five

After the official stuff was finished, I followed Trent to a pizza place where we pigged out on a huge pizza with lots of pepperoni. One cannot live on chocolate alone. Trust me. I've tried.

As we sat in the crowded, noisy restaurant savoring the smells and flavors, I made a joke about my middle-of-the-night adventure. "There I was, armed with a rolling pin, following my psycho cat into the basement, chasing a mouse." I laughed then took another bite of pizza and waited for Trent to laugh, to make light of the entire episode, to assure me I was being silly so I could quit feeling weird about it.

He didn't laugh. Didn't even crack a smile as he slowly lowered his piece of pizza to his plate, his eyes never leaving my face. "Lindsay, you need to know about this little service we have in town. If you hear noises in the night, you can punch in three numbers on your phone, 911, and a big brave cop with a gun instead of a rolling pin will come and investigate. It's been known to save lives."

"Save lives? I had no idea you'd be so worried about a mouse. But you don't need to be concerned. Even if I'd found the little critter, my aim is so bad, I wouldn't have been able to hit him with that rolling pin."

Trent looked across the room then back to me and shook his head. "You're dating…I mean, seeing…I mean…whatever it is we're doing. You're involved with a cop, but you don't think to call one when something scary happens in the middle of the night?"

I rolled my eyes. "Nothing scary happened! You're overreacting. If I called 911 about something like that, I can just hear your buddies when you came in to work the next morning. *Hey, Trent, got a call to Lindsay's house last night! Seems she had a mouse B&E. We put handcuffs on him, but his arms were so little, they slipped right out!*"

Trent lifted his hands in a gesture of surrender. "Have it your way. But I was there a few months ago when they were pumping your stomach because somebody broke into your house and tried to kill you."

That memory had certainly crossed my mind last night, but I wasn't going to admit it. "That was Paula's psycho ex. He's in prison, and nobody's been breaking into my house lately."

Trent nodded. "Fine." He lifted his pizza and resumed eating. So did I.

"I should probably get a gun," I said after a couple of bites of silence.

"Probably not."

We ate some more.

"You could teach me to shoot," I said.

"Probably not."

"I could take a class."

Trent swallowed his last bite of pizza, drank the last of his soda, and wiped his hands on a napkin. "That's not a bad idea."

I hadn't expected that response.

"As soon as you're divorced from Rick, I'll help you find a gun and a class."

"Why do I have to wait until I'm divorced from Rick-head?"

"So you don't lose your temper and shoot him."

"He deserves shooting."

"Yes, he does, but if you get sent to prison, that's going to put a real damper on our spending time together."

He had a point. Still, I'd love to see Rick's face if he came to my door and I greeted him with a .357 Magnum. *Do you feel lucky, Rick? Well, do you? Go ahead. Make my day.*

"Stop fantasizing about killing Rick, finish your pizza, and let's go to your house."

Trent followed me home. I put my car in my stylishly angled garage and we walked over to the porch. I let Henry out to join us since Trent's his buddy. After Henry wound around my legs and Trent's, he left to patrol his territory. I have no idea how far his territory ranges, but I haven't seen another cat in the area since Henry arrived.

I sat down in the porch swing. It was a beautiful night with a spectacular moon, and Trent is a spectacular kisser. "Want to make out?"

He turned to me, the moonlight shadows settling into concerned lines on his face. I sighed. We probably weren't going to make out.

"Yes," he said. "After we check your basement."

Oh, well, if that was all it took. "Sure. Come on. I just hope you weren't planning to wear those clothes ever again because you'll never be able to get them clean."

"You don't even want to know some of the places these clothes have been."

He was right. I didn't.

We trekked through the house and down the stairs to the furnace room. I turned on the overhead bulb, and Trent produced a large, deadly looking flashlight. It lit up the room like the sun and looked at least as effective as a rolling pin in terms of a weapon.

He shone the light all around the room, studying every inch of it carefully, then walked over to the corner where the bricks seemed to be the most disturbed. Squatting...and getting coal dust all over his pants...he picked up some of the sediment between his fingers, tested it, put it back down and ran his fingers over the uneven surface of the bricks.

"You are never going to be clean again," I warned him.

He stood, grinned, walked over to me and drew a grimy finger down my cheek, then kissed me.

I scrubbed at the streak on my face. "I'd have had to hurt you if you hadn't thrown in the kiss."

"I know." Then he looked serious, turned back to the room and swept his light over the area. "It looks like somebody's been digging up your floor fairly recently."

Again he was saying things I didn't want to hear. "Stop being a paranoid cop."

"Lindsay, it's possible you had an intruder last night, a two-legged intruder, not a four-legged critter." The dead calm in his voice told me he wasn't feeling at all calm about this.

"No, it's not possible. I checked the doors and windows, and they were all locked."

He strode over to the boarded-up coal chute and repeated my inspection of the night before, pushing and tugging on each board to be sure it was securely in place.

I folded my arms and glared at him. "I already did that."

"Mmm-hmm." He continued checking it out as if I hadn't spoken, then finally stepped back and gave me another serious look. "There's some evidence of disturbance around these boards. Let's go outside and look at the entrance."

I shivered. "I got a better idea. Let's go outside and sit in the porch swing and make out and talk about what we're going to do when my divorce is final."

He smiled, the corners of his eyes crinkling as he switched off the flashlight and came over to me. Putting his arms around me, he leaned close to my ear. I thought the discussion about the phantom intruder was finished.

"Just as soon as we check out the coal chute entrance," he whispered.

That man is almost as stubborn as I am.

We went upstairs, and I took him out back to the alley. We pushed through my overgrown shrubbery, and I showed him the ornate metal door that had covered the coal chute since the house was built.

He lifted the big, rusty padlock that held the door securely closed and looked at it. "Where's the key?"

"I have no idea. I haven't had to open it recently for a delivery of coal."

He tugged on the lock a couple of times, let it drop, then felt around the edges of the door carefully. "You didn't get a key from the former owner when you bought the house?"

I shrugged. "Rick took care of all those details. When I moved in here last year, he gave me the door keys. I had all those locks changed last winter and threw away the old keys. The key to this one could have been in that bunch. You really are being a little paranoid, don't you think?"

He took my hand and we started back around to the front of the house. "I'm a cop. Paranoid is what I do. I have to keep you safe long enough to take you up on some of those post-divorce promises."

We had just settled into the porch swing when a car door slammed. We both stood and looked toward the street.

A dark green SUV.

Rick.

"Lindsay!" Clad in white knit shirt and white tennis shorts, he charged down the sidewalk and onto my porch.

From out of nowhere, Henry darted up, putting himself between Rick and me, his back arched, tail high, teeth bared. He doesn't like Rick and feels the need to protect me from him. If only he'd been around five years ago. *If anyone has reason why this man and this woman should not be married...* ROWR!

"Rick. What are you doing here?"

Rick glared at Trent, and Trent glared at Rick. Neither spoke.

Henry hissed. Smart cat.

Rick turned his gaze to me. "I came to see how you're doing. I heard you got called in for questioning too."

"I did, yes, but since I'm not dating the victim's wife, my interview was pretty simple and nonthreatening."

Rick ducked his head as if embarrassed. He wasn't, of course. He never is. "That's what I need to talk to you about." He sent another glare in Trent's direction.

Trent squeezed my hand then released it. "I better go. I'll talk to you tomorrow." He knew from previous experience that if he stayed, Rick would get crazier and crazier.

I wouldn't have minded if the two of them got into a fight because I knew Trent could beat Rick to a bloody pulp, but Trent has all these lofty notions about keeping his job and staying out of jail and that sort of thing.

"You don't have to go," I said. "Rick's leaving."

"No, I'm not."

"Yes, you are."

"Lindsay, we need to talk. I'm ready to sign those papers."

I wasn't sure I'd heard right. "*Those* papers? Which papers?"

"The divorce papers, of course."

Trent and I shared a look of disbelief. "Do you want me to stay?" he asked.

If there was even a chance that Rick really meant it this time, I had to take that chance.

"No, it's okay."

Rick let him go with a curt nod but no sarcastic remark. That was different and, I thought, a good sign.

I waved as Trent drove away, then I turned back to Rick. "Okay, you're ready to sign the papers. When do you want to meet with the lawyers and get that done?"

He walked over and sat down in the swing. "Whenever you say."

I remained standing with King Henry beside me. "I'll call my lawyer tomorrow, and he'll call your lawyer and schedule an appointment. That's settled. You can leave now."

Rick smiled, draped an arm across the back of the swing and stretched out his tan legs. "Come sit next to me, babe."

"No."

He stepped up the wattage on his smile. "I'm sorry we've had so much trouble getting this resolved, Lindsay." Rick was apologizing? That was a bad sign. It could only mean he was working a

59

scam. "It's been hard for me to give you up, but I've come to realize, if I really love you, I need to let you go."

I looked upward, expecting the sky to fall or a bolt of lightning to strike after such an outrageous lie. "Fine, whatever. I'll call my lawyer, and he'll call your lawyer. Good-bye."

Rick's smile developed sad overtones. "I'm trying to make things right, Lindsay. Please let me do that."

Henry, making a soft growling sound, sidled closer to Rick.

Rick shifted as if the swing had suddenly become uncomfortable. "Why is that cat looking at me like that?"

"He's psychic. He knows what's going on in that demented mind of yours, what your real agenda is. You're not going to sign those papers, are you?"

"Yes, I am. I just want to do what's best for you. Lindsay, I'm a changed man." He drew in a deep breath. "I've fallen in love."

Henry turned his head and looked at me. He didn't believe what he'd just heard either.

"No, you haven't," I said. "You're not capable of love. You're too shallow."

He didn't even rise to the bait, just kept smiling like he was stoned. Maybe he was.

"I understand why you'd think that, but this time it's the real thing."

"You said that about Muffy and Becky and Vanessa and—"

"This is different."

Suddenly it hit me. "You're not talking about Rodney Bradford's widow, are you?"

He gave that doper smile again. "Yes, I am talking about Lisa."

I shook my head in disbelief and sank to the top step. "This sounds like one of those television shows about sleazy people! You were having an affair with your client's wife, and now that he's dead, you're suddenly in love with her?"

Rick came over to sit beside me. "You make it sound so tawdry! Lisa and I were drawn to each other the first time she came into my office."

"That would be when she came in with her husband?"

"Yes, with her husband, but he wasn't a very good husband."

"I'm familiar with that syndrome."

For an instant Rick looked as if he might be going to respond, but then that phony smile came back. "I know I wasn't a good husband, but I'm trying to make it up to you now. At least I didn't beat you like Rodney beat poor little Lisa."

"Poor little Lisa?"

"Rodney's not who you think he is. He just got out of prison a couple of months ago. Lisa was trying to help him rehabilitate, but he just couldn't escape his past. It was probably one of his criminal buddies who killed him. He was a terrible man."

I decided against admitting I already knew about the terrible man's scenic past. "How awful for poor little Lisa. Thank goodness she's got a fine man like you now."

61

"I know I haven't always been the best person, but I'm trying to make up for the wrong things I've done." Rick was definitely up to something, and I'd bet my next month's profits at Death by Chocolate that it didn't involve falling madly in love with poor little Lisa.

"That's commendable. I'm thrilled for you, and I wish you both the best. Once our divorce is finalized, you can marry her and live happily ever after. I'll call my lawyer in the morning."

I stood and waited, but he didn't get up to leave. I hadn't expected him to.

"That's big of you, Lindsay, but you always have been a decent person."

"I won't argue with that."

"I feel so bad about all the wrong I've done. I want to make it up to you for the times I cheated and lied and took advantage of you."

"Give me a divorce, and we'll call it even. I absolve you of all guilt." I waved my hands through the air. "Veni, vidi, vici." It was the only Latin I knew. "Absolution granted. No bad karma for you as you go through the rest of your life. Just sign the freaking papers!"

Finally he stood. I stepped back. Henry, too, got out of his way.

He leaned over to hug me.

I drew back. "Don't do that."

He nodded, tried to look abashed, and stepped down to the sidewalk. Then he turned back. "Let me just do this one thing for you so I can ease my conscience. Instead of me taking the big house and you this little one, I'm going to let you have the nice house and I'll take this one."

Aha! "I don't want your house! I want this one!" All of a sudden, everybody wanted my house.

"The big one's worth a lot more. If you don't want to live there, you can sell it and buy another house. Buy the one across the street so you can still be close to Paula and Fred."

I folded my arms and raised an eyebrow. "Really? Live across the street from you and Lisa? That would be cozy."

For an instant, an expression of *damn, I screwed up* flickered across Rick's face. But only for an instant. Someone who didn't know him as well as I would have missed it. "Okay, maybe that wasn't a good suggestion. It was just a thought. The point is, you'll have lots of options."

I shook my head. "Give it a rest. You don't plan to live here. Why do you want my house?"

"I just want to do the right thing."

I clutched the porch railing in anticipation of a major earthquake that would swallow us all. "If you want to do the right thing, sign those papers exactly as they are and get out of my life!"

Rick held up his hands in a defensive gesture. "Okay, okay. Besides my wanting to do the right thing, Lisa wants to have this place because it meant so much to Rodney."

I threw my arms into the air in total frustration. "Poor little Lisa wants to own a house where the man who abused her used to visit his grandparents? You are so full of it, Richard Kramer!"

I stormed into my house…which was going to remain my house for the foreseeable future…and slammed the door behind me then opened it again to let Henry inside. He marched in with his usual regal grace, giving his long tail a switch, bidding a haughty farewell to Rick.

"Lindsay," Rick said, no longer smiling, "I'm trying to do the right thing. Don't fight me on this or things are going to get ugly."

"You're about nine years late with that prediction." I slammed the door again.

# Chapter Six

For a few moments I leaned against the door, steaming, until I heard Rick's car drive away. Henry wound around my leg and purred loudly. Gradually my breathing slowed and the anger went down a few notches. Amazing how a little feline affection can calm the nervous system.

I leaned over and lifted him into my arms, grateful for the comfort. He allowed me to cuddle him for a few seconds, then squirmed away and trotted off to the kitchen. I followed. He deserved a treat for threatening Rick.

I refilled Henry's bowl of dry food then opened a can of tuna and gave him half. He purred and ate at the same time. The only thing he likes better than tuna is catnip. I considered some of that too, but didn't want a drunk watch cat if somebody really was trying to break into my house.

While Henry dined, I called Fred.

"Were you asleep?" I asked, suddenly realizing it was almost ten o'clock. Not that he's ever been asleep any time I've called. Wouldn't surprise me to learn he's figured out a way to eliminate the need for sleep.

"No. Were you?"

"I wish. If I were, that would make this entire evening just a bad nightmare." I told him about everything...my previous night's adventure, Trent's suspicions and Rick's visit.

"Curious, this sudden interest in your house. It sat on the market for several months before you bought it, and you haven't made any significant improvements since then."

"Hey! You don't need to be rude."

"I'm just being factual."

"Maybe I have buried treasure in the basement and somebody just found the secret map."

"That's not likely."

"Then why is my house suddenly such a hot property?"

"It's not your landscaping."

"For your information, the CIA called just the other day wanting to use my yard to train their jungle operatives."

"I hope you said *no*. Let the CIA in, and the whole neighborhood goes downhill."

I never know for sure when he's kidding.

"Would you see what you can find out about the people we bought this house from, Rodney's grandparents? Where they went from here, how they died, that sort of thing. I think their name was Murray. They seemed like really nice, normal people, but maybe they were eccentric and buried a fortune in the furnace room in the basement."

"That's extremely unlikely, but even if they did, how would I find out anything about it?"

"I'll make you your very own fresh-out-of-the-oven triple chocolate chip cookies with chopped hazelnuts if you'll find out what the heck is going on with my house."

He didn't hesitate. "Okay."

I assumed he was going to hang up without saying good-bye, as he's prone to do, and had my own receiver halfway to the phone when I heard him speaking again.

"Lock the door to your basement tonight."

If everybody was trying to comfort and reassure me about my safety, they were all doing a pretty lousy job of it. "So you think it was a person, not a mouse, in my basement last night?"

"Probably a mouse."

"Then why should I lock my door?"

"You want mice in your house?"

He hung up.

Like I said, I never know if he's being serious or kidding.

I locked the basement door then set a kitchen chair under the knob. Can't be too careful when you're dealing with mice.

\*\*\*

Paula told me the next morning that we had made the ten o'clock news. They'd featured some great pictures of the cops being interviewed with my sign in full view, and the reporter had mentioned that the dead man's final act before collapsing on the sidewalk had been to eat dessert at "a local restaurant, Death by Chocolate. Appropriate name."

I considered the alternatives…prepare small quantities of everything and pretend all was normal or admit it was far from normal and go with the flow. I chose the latter and made brownies with nuts, dark chocolate chips, semi-sweet chocolate chips and white chocolate chips then layered on thick chocolate frosting and called our special dessert of the day *Killer Chocolate*.

I made the right choice. We had a big crowd for breakfast and a huge crowd for lunch. Everyone wanted to know what dessert the murdered man had eaten. I finally drew a line through *Killer Chocolate* and wrote above it *Murdered Man's Brownies*. Okay, it was a little macabre, but we sold out. It's not my fault if people are strange. I don't judge. I just feed them chocolate.

I arrived home around 3:00 exhausted but happy. The shop was thriving in spite of The Incident, I'd had no more night time visitors, and I was no worse off than before with regard to my divorce.

I refilled Henry's bowl and caved in to his demands for more tuna. The can was already open, and I wasn't going to eat any of it. "Maybe we'll have some catnip tonight," I promised, "since you don't need to be on guard."

The phone rang. It was Fred. "We're going to visit the Murrays," he said.

"At the cemetery?"

"No, at Summerdale Retirement Village."

"They're not dead?" I sank onto a wooden chair at my kitchen table. I shouldn't be surprised to find no morsel of truth in anything Rick told me.

"Not even close. They've been on the golf course this afternoon, and there's a dance at the Village Center tonight, but they can squeeze in a couple of hours if we hurry."

"What did you tell them?"

"I didn't tell them their grandson died after eating at your restaurant, nor did I tell you think there's buried treasure in the basement. I simply told them you'd moved into the place and would like to visit with them about a couple of things."

"And they agreed?"

"Without hesitation. They remember you and thought you were a lovely person. That's Mrs. Murray's word, not mine."

Suddenly I felt a little silly. "What are we going to talk about if I can't ask her about the pirate gold in the basement?"

"I didn't say you couldn't ask her. I just said I didn't mention it. I think this is a good place to start figuring out what Rick wants with your house. I'd suggest cookies as a conversation starter."

"For the Murrays or you?"

"All of us." He hung up.

Fortunately I had a few chocolate chip cookies from the day before. I hoped the Murrays weren't allergic to nuts or gluten.

\*\*\*

We drove across town to Summerdale Retirement Village in Fred's pristine white 1968 Mercedes. Although he doesn't like to let anyone ride in his special car, he hates even more to ride in mine which is generally messy and has me for a driver. He

69

claims my driving gives him a heart attack. He only rode with me one time, and he survived just fine, though he did crawl out and cross himself as soon as I stopped.

"You drive too slow," I told him, just to keep things even. "I find it extremely stressful. I could have a heart attack."

"I'm going exactly the speed limit."

"Thank you for making my point."

The grounds of Summerdale were green and well-tended with lots of trees and open areas around the one-story tidy beige buildings trimmed in white. Fred drove without hesitation through the winding streets of the complex to Building 14, Unit C. I think somewhere in his past he had a GPS chip implanted in his brain, though I'm sure he reprogrammed it to delete that annoying *recalculating* woman.

Unit C was small but bright and immaculate, and Mr. and Mrs. Murray were just as I remembered them. She was short with snow white hair curling gently around a pink-cheeked, cheerful face. He was taller than she though not a lot and had twinkling blue eyes behind thick glasses and a full head of the same white hair as his wife. I suppose age is the great equalizer of hair color.

We shook hands all around, and I introduced Fred.

"Can I get you something to drink? I just made a fresh pot of coffee and a pitcher of iced tea."

"Thank you," I said. "I'd love a glass of tea, and Fred would like some coffee. I brought you some cookies."

"Why, thank you! Did you ever open that chocolate bakery you were talking about?"

Nothing wrong with her memory.

"I did." I started to mention the name of my place but didn't want to open the conversation with the fact that her grandson died at my restaurant.

"Good for you. I'll be right back with those drinks."

"Have a seat," Mr. Murray invited.

Fred and I sat on the muted rose sofa, and Mr. Murray took one of the matching chairs. The room had a feeling of serenity, or maybe it was just the occupants of the room. I could see no resemblance between the Murrays and Rodney Bradford. He must have taken after his father's side of the family.

"You're not the same young man we met before," Murray said, studying Fred through the thick lenses of his glasses.

"No, this is my neighbor. You met my ex-husband, Rick."

Murray arched a shaggy white eyebrow. "Ex? Good decision. I didn't much like that guy. Seemed sneaky."

I laughed. "You're perceptive. He is sneaky."

Mrs. Murray returned from the kitchen with a tray holding a plate with the cookies on it, three cups of coffee and one Coke. She set the tray on the coffee table and smiled at me. "I remembered you liked Coca-Cola so I brought one instead of iced tea. I can change it if you'd like."

"No, Coke is great. Thank you." Definitely no senility happening there.

71

She handed her husband a cup of coffee and a cookie then settled in the other arm chair with her own drink and snack.

"So you're living in our old house," she said. "Oh my, this cookie is delicious! You need to tell me where your bakery is so I can come there. Isn't this the best cookie you've ever eaten, Harold?"

"Good, but not better than yours, sweet-pea." He grinned and winked at me.

Cathy rolled her eyes, but she smiled.

"Yes," I said, wanting to avoid the subject of the name of my restaurant as long as possible, "I'm living in your old house, and I just love it."

"She's divorcing that sneaky guy," Harold supplied.

"Good. I like this one much better."

"Oh, no, Fred's not...he's my friend, my neighbor. You lived next door to him for about a year."

"Of course! You're the one with the closed curtains."

"I am. I don't go outside often."

"You should. You're much too pale. Sunshine's good for you. Harold and I go bicycling and play golf, and in the winter we go to Texas for a few months."

"Chasing the sunshine," Harold said. "Feels good on these old bones."

A moment of silence ensued. The proprieties had been observed. It was time to get down to the reason for our visit.

"Did you have a key for that big padlock on the coal chute door?" I asked.

"Why, yes, I'm sure we did. We put that lock on when we moved in. Somebody could have come inside that way. Didn't we give you that key with the others when we closed on the house?"

"I'm sure you did. Rick didn't pass it on to me, but that's okay. I have no need to unlock it. Haven't had any coal deliveries in a while."

Harold and Cathy both laughed but looked a little puzzled at the turn the conversation had taken.

Fred set his cup on the coffee table. He had a look about him that said he was going to say something momentous. "We were very sorry to hear about your grandson."

The loudest silence I ever heard filled every inch of that cheerful little room.

Cathy looked at Harold.

Harold looked at Cathy.

They appeared to be upset, but not grief-stricken.

"How did you hear about our grandson?" Cathy asked quietly.

I clutched my Coke tightly. "I'm so sorry! He was killed outside my restaurant."

The Murrays exchanged looks again.

"George isn't dead," Harold said.

"George? Who's George? I'm talking about Rodney."

"Who's Rodney?"

We all sat and looked at each other for a few long moments.

73

"Could your grandson have been using an assumed name?" Fred asked.

Cathy shifted in her chair, looked at her hands in her lap, then finally lifted her chin. "Our grandson used a lot of assumed names, but now he only has a name and number. He's in prison and will be for another eight years. Well, maybe less with good behavior, and he is a good boy."

# Chapter Seven

"Rodney Bradford just got out of prison. Are you sure your grandson is still there?" I regretted the callous words the minute they came out of my mouth, especially when I saw the uncomfortable way Harold and Cathy looked.

"We're sure," Harold said softly.

"George's life didn't turn out the way we hoped it would, but he's still our grandson. We love him. We stay in touch with him. Why would you think this other man was our grandson?"

I shrugged. "He told me he was. He said he wanted to buy my house because he used to visit his grandparents there when he was a boy."

Cathy looked puzzled. "We lived in that house for forty years, raised our family there. George did come to visit sometimes, but nobody named Rodney Bradford."

"Do you have a picture of George?" Fred asked.

Cathy lifted a framed photograph from the lamp table beside her. Fred stood and took it from her then sat back down and held it so we could both look at it.

A small boy stood between smiling parents. I had no idea whether he resembled Rodney Bradford. At that age, it could have been a picture of any little kid, even Fred, assuming he'd ever been that young.

"Do you have a more recent picture?" I asked.

"Not really," Cathy said. "After he started getting in trouble, he didn't want his picture taken. That's him when he was nine, and our son, John, with his wife, Tina. That was taken just before John died in an automobile accident. The boy never stood a chance with just Tina to raise him."

"She wasn't a bad person," Harold said.

Cathy nodded. "That's true. She was a good person, but she wasn't strong. John was the strong one, the care-giver. He was always bringing home stray dogs and cats and birds. He wanted to take care of the world."

"He wanted to take care of Tina."

Cathy nodded again. "John saw so much potential in her, he just wanted to help her. They dated in high school. That's when she got on drugs the first time. John had her in and out of rehab more than once. If he'd lived, I think she would have made it."

"She would have made it," Harold agreed.

"But she married that awful man before John's body was cold in the ground, and he got her back into drugs."

*That awful man.* We'd finally found someone the genial, forgiving Murrays didn't like.

"We tried to help her with George." Harold shook his head, his expression morose. "Anything we did, they undid. She and that man didn't want to be bothered with George. They let him run wild, do whatever he wanted as long as they didn't have to sober up and take some responsibility. George was in trouble every time you turned around."

"What kind of trouble?" Fred asked.

"All kinds," Cathy said. "Fights at school—"

"When he bothered to go to school," Harold added darkly.

"He dropped out when he was fifteen and joined one of those gangs, the Crickets or Coffins or something like that. Tina died of a drug overdose a few years later. George was nineteen then, and he seemed to straighten up for a while, like he suddenly realized where he was headed."

"That didn't last long," Harold muttered.

"No, it didn't. We were able to get him out of scrapes when he was a teenager, but after he turned twenty-one, it was a lot harder. We hired a lawyer this last time, but he'd been in so much trouble already, the best we could do was get him a lighter sentence."

"What was he convicted of?" Fred asked.

"Possession of drugs with the intent to sell them." Cathy sat stiffly erect and spoke the words with concise precision, as if she'd memorized them from a foreign language without fully comprehending their meaning.

I felt kind of bad that we'd forced these nice people to relive so much sadness.

Fred obviously didn't. "If you had to pay for George's defense, apparently he wasn't very successful as a drug dealer."

Cathy dropped her gaze to the floor. "I think he sampled his own wares too often."

"So he never had a large sum of money in his possession?" Fred asked. I would have never asked that question. It seemed rude. Good thing Fred was there to do it for me.

Cathy smiled sadly and reached for her husband's hand. "If George had ever come into any money, he'd have offered to pay us back for all the money we spent on him over the years. He's a good boy."

"A good boy," Harold echoed. "Weak, but he has a good heart. He always wanted to do the right thing. He just couldn't quite get there."

We took our leave of the Murrays, promising to stay in touch, and they promised to visit Death by Chocolate often. I suspected they would. They really liked my cookies.

We settled into Fred's car and drove away from quiet Summerdale.

"I like them," I said. "They seem content and at peace with the world. Getting old doesn't sound so bad if I can do it like the Murrays."

Fred snorted. "Not likely. You're much too pushy and abrasive to ever be peaceful and content with your life."

I wanted to argue with that assessment, but I couldn't. "That's so sweet that they still think their convict grandson is a nice boy," I said instead.

"They're naïve."

"Same difference. What do you make of all this? Think Rodney Bradford is really their grandson George?"

For a few minutes Fred focused on the road ahead, deftly but slowly navigating through the traffic as if that was his only concern, but I knew the bits and bytes in the computer that passed for his brain were spinning at warp speed. "Maybe," he finally said. "The two of them could have somehow switched identities so George got released instead of Rodney. That would be quite a trick, but stranger things have happened in the prison system. When I get home I'll look up his mug shot, and we'll see who's who."

"If Rodney turns out to be George, it could be that he buried some drug money in his grandparents' basement, and that's why he wanted my house, to get it back." I twisted in my seat, turning to face him, excited at finding something that made sense. "And that would explain why his wife...widow...wants my house! He told her about the money. I'll bet she's the one who killed him!"

He frowned. "Why would she kill him?"

"I don't know. Maybe he really did beat her, and she just decided to get rid of him so she wouldn't have to share the money with a wife-beater."

"Then why didn't she wait until they got the money before killing him?"

I sat back against the plush white leather. "I don't know. Okay, forget that idea. Can you come up with something better?"

A car pulled from a side street right in front of Fred. He slowed with no change of expression and without uttering a single swear word. "I don't have enough data to form an opinion at this time.

However, you could be right about George burying money in your basement. I think we need to dig up the floor in your furnace room."

I wasn't sure I'd heard correctly. I turned toward Fred and studied his implacable profile, looking for any trace of a smile, any hint he was kidding. There was none. "You want to dig a hole in my basement?"

"I can't think of another way to find out if there's something of value buried there. If we were looking for gold or some other form of metal or if we knew that what we're looking for was buried in a metal box, we could use a detector. But we don't have any idea what we're looking for, so the only reasonable solution is to dig up the floor in your furnace room."

"Oh yeah, sure, that sounds like a perfectly reasonable solution."

"Good."

Sometimes Fred fails to recognize sarcasm. Or he ignores it.

"When do you want to undertake this excavation?" I asked, hoping for a date in the distant future.

"When do you want to figure out if you've got a mouse or a human intruder and why everybody wants your house?"

I wasn't crazy about spending another night worrying if I had an intruder, two-legged or four-legged, in the basement. "Tonight?" On the other hand, I wasn't crazy about spending an hour or two in the basement doing manual labor. "Or in a week or so."

Fred stared at the road ahead, turned a corner and finally nodded. "We can get started tonight. This may take a while. You should probably make more cookies. Digging is hard work."

***

I changed into old jeans and a tee-shirt in preparation for braving the coal dust and had just taken a pan of freshly-baked cookies from the oven when I heard a knock on my back door.

I knew it had to be Fred, but it was getting dark outside and my life had been a little scary the last couple of days. For a moment I stood in the middle of the kitchen balancing the cookie sheet, wavering between hanging onto that hot pan as a weapon or setting it on the counter and picking up my rolling pin.

Henry dozed under the table, his body inside a paper bag with his head sticking out. I bought him a nice kitty bed, but he prefers boxes, sacks, drawers, and, of course, my bed. He opened one blue eye, regarded me quizzically, closed that eye and gave a soft snore. If he wasn't snarling and threatening to attack my caller, there was no danger.

I set the cookies on the counter and opened the back door.

Fred, wearing coveralls, stood on the stoop. He had a shovel in each hand and a canvas bag hanging over one arm.

"You scared me. Why did you come to the back door?" I asked, though I had no hope of getting a reasonable reply.

"Why would I go to the front door when you're in the kitchen?"

Actually, that did sound reasonable.

"Come on in." I stepped back so he could enter with his tools.

"George Murray and Rodney Bradford are not the same person, but they were cellmates."

"Hack into the state prison records tonight?"

He ignored my question. "Can't be a coincidence. Maybe George hid money in this house and told Bradford about it. Cellmates can become close friends in the restrictive arena of prison."

The possibility of hidden treasure in my basement suddenly became real. "If we find money, do we have to give it back?"

Fred thought for a moment. "Probably." He turned and headed for the basement door but paused at the pan of cookies. "Chopped hazelnuts?"

"Yes."

Henry reached out a paw and lazily swiped at Fred's leg. Fred ignored him and continued to the basement.

I locked the back door and followed Fred.

We made our way down to the suddenly-popular furnace room, and I flipped on the light. From his bag Fred produced a very bright light on a folding tripod which lit up the room like the midday sun in August. It was even brighter than Trent's super flashlight. If there was so much as a needle hidden in that room, we'd find it.

"First," he said, "we remove the bricks from that area in the corner."

Trent had seemed interested in that area too, and I'd thought it looked more disturbed than the rest of the floor when I did my inspection. Perhaps we were onto something.

Fred dipped into his bag and brought out two pairs of leather gloves and two tools that looked sort of like spatulas. I put on gloves and took a spatula. "What do you call this thing?" I asked.

"Spatula."

"Oh."

We began to take up the bricks using the spatulas. They came out surprisingly easily, and I was getting excited, expecting at any moment to see the flash of gold.

An hour or a week later, depending on whether you measure time by the clock or by the torture involved, I was less excited. We'd moved bricks from about half the floor and dug through several inches of the black clay underneath to find...more black clay.

I was thrilled when Fred stopped digging and leaned on his shovel. "I think we've learned all we're going to learn."

"Well, I've learned that if I ever kill Rick, I'm going to dispose of his body some way other than burying him, so I suppose it hasn't been a totally wasted evening." I laid down my shovel and pulled off my gloves.

"What are you doing?"

"Quitting. What are you doing?"

"Getting ready to put the floor back the way it was when we came down here, only we'll smooth it out as long as we're here anyway."

I looked around at the piles of bricks and dirt. "Forget it. Let's go eat cookies. I never use this room."

Fred began spreading the dirt around evenly. "Neither of us will be able to sleep tonight if we don't get this room back in order before we leave it."

"I could sleep," I assured him.

"No, you couldn't. Thinking about this mess would keep me awake, and I'd be banging on your door, demanding we tidy up this room. As I said, neither of us would be able to sleep."

I glared at him but started moving dirt and bricks.

Fred produced a level from his canvas bag and used that on the floor before we reset the bricks. Mr. Perfection. Finally the room looked better than it had when we started.

He stepped to one side and surveyed our efforts. "We ought to take up the whole floor and smooth it out."

"Not tonight."

"All right. Get a broom, we'll sweep up the dust and dirt and be finished down here."

I lifted my shovel threateningly. "A broom? Sweep the floor? Now?"

He wasn't threatened. "Yes. Want me to go upstairs and get it?"

"No."

I started upstairs.

"Bring a duster for these cobwebs."

I got the broom and the duster, and we cleaned the furnace room.

"I hope you'll be able to get a good night's sleep now," I said when we finished.

"I will."

We climbed the stairs, and I locked the basement door behind me.

Henry was gone, his paper bag empty. He was probably waiting for me in my bed. Well, he was probably in my bed. As to whether he was waiting for me, whether he cared if I joined him or not, that's always an open question with a cat.

Fred crossed my white vinyl kitchen leaving dark footprints. I hoped he wouldn't notice and insist we clean them up that night before he could sleep.

"Bring the cookies, and let's sit on the back stoop and talk," he said.

"Why don't we sit in here where the cookies already are and the air conditioning works?"

"Because we're filthy. We're already leaving tracks on your floor. You'll probably have to mop before you go to bed."

"Yeah, I'll do that." *Right after I mop and wax the sidewalk in front of my house.*

I put some cookies on a plate, grabbed two Cokes, turned off the kitchen light and followed Fred outside.

We sat on the steps of my back porch eating and drinking for a few minutes. The night was pleasant, still hot but comfortable with the sun no longer blazing. The moon hadn't risen yet, and it was very dark. I looked around at the trees and the out-of-control shrubbery surrounding my house. In the daylight I loved the lush greenery and the shade it gave me. In the dark it was a little spooky.

"Take this." Fred extended his hand toward me. Even in the darkness I could see the shiny key on his palm. "I put a new padlock on that coal chute door," he said.

I accepted the key. "Thank you. But—you don't really think somebody climbed through there to get into my basement, do you?"

He looked at me silently for a moment, took a long swallow from his can of Coke and set it back down. "We need to talk about what we discovered tonight."

"Fred, I was there. We discovered nothing but how hard the ground is."

"One area was easier to dig."

"Maybe that area in the corner was a little softer," I admitted.

"As if the ground had been loosened recently."

Damn. I didn't like where this conversation was going. I grabbed my own Coke and tilted it to my mouth...but it was empty. Thank goodness I had a fresh twelve-pack in the refrigerator.

"I think someone got into your basement and dug up whatever was there. When I cut off your old padlock and opened that metal door, I found a latching mechanism that releases the wooden cover that blocks the opening on the inside. Somebody could release it, let it down, slide into your basement, then climb back up again and pull that interior door closed."

The temperature was probably in the mid-eighties, but that image sent big time shivers down my spine. "Damn! Henry was right! Somebody was in my house."

"Anyone who had access to the key to that padlock could have entered your basement at any time."

I shivered again then started to get angry as the implications of that set in. "George could have buried drug money in his grandparents' basement, hidden the key to the padlock, then told his cellmate, Bradford. Or the Murrays could have given that padlock key to Rick when we bought this house, and he kept it and used it after he found out from his client, the late Rodney Bradford, about the money buried there." I wasn't sure if I preferred to think Rick or some stranger had been in my basement. Both possibilities were creepy.

"I don't think it's Rick since he tried to get your house after the intrusion occurred."

"Oh."

"And Bradford was dead by that time."

"So who was in my house?"

Fred shrugged. "I have no idea. It's possible whoever was there found nothing and still needs access to your house to search further, so we can't completely eliminate Rick."

"We can't eliminate anybody in this entire city except Rodney Bradford. I don't think my clean furnace room is going to help me sleep tonight.

Doesn't make me feel even a little bit better to know an intruder won't get his feet dirty."

# Chapter Eight

I hate getting up early, but there's something cozy about being awake and working with a friend during those predawn hours. Paula and I have some of our best talks while it's still dark outside and we're inside preparing for the breakfast crowd.

I told her about the previous evening's excavations, and she told me I was insane.

"It's dangerous for you to remain in that house right now. Why don't you stay with me until they catch Bradford's murderer? Zach would like having his Anlinny sleep over. You could bring Henry. Zach loves that cat."

I shrugged and added a little extra chocolate to my chocolate nut bread. "Whatever attraction was in the furnace room in my basement is gone now. Nothing down there but dirt and bricks. Not even any dust or cobwebs. No reason for somebody to come back."

"Just because you and Fred didn't find something doesn't mean there's nothing there. As far as you knew a few days ago, there wasn't any reason for somebody to break into your house in the first place." She measured grounds into the coffee maker and shook her head. "I don't like it. A man was murdered while trying to buy your house, and now you find out somebody was inside searching for something. Pretty hard to believe that's a coincidence. The murder and your house must be related."

The same conclusion Fred had reached.

I put the loaves of nut bread in the oven and started on the cookies. "You're right. This all started with Rick bringing that man into my life. I'm going to call him and demand some answers."

Paula snorted in a very unladylike manner and slapped the switch to start the coffee brewing. "You think you're going to get anything out of Rick? Why don't you call Trent? He's investigating the murder and he has an interest in keeping you safe. Rick's only interest is in taking advantage of you."

"That's true, but it's nothing personal with him. Rick's only interest in anybody is taking advantage of them. I wonder where his new girlfriend fits into this picture."

A timer dinged, and Paula removed a large pan of cinnamon rolls from the oven. They weren't chocolate, but they certainly did smell good. "Money," she said. "Maybe Lisa was the money behind Bradford's offer to buy your house. She has money, and Rick's planning to get his share of it."

I added chocolate chips to my cookies and then ate a handful. Have to run periodic tests on those chips, make sure they're fresh. "That doesn't explain why he and Lisa wanted my house. What if Lisa got the information about the treasure in my house from Bradford and then she killed him and now Rick's blackmailing her to get the information so he can get more than just a real estate commission on the deal? You're right. I need to talk to Trent just in case he hasn't thought of that possibility."

\*\*\*

I called Trent on my way home from work that afternoon. Yeah, yeah, I know talking on a cell phone while driving isn't a good idea. But I have Bluetooth, and I didn't really expect him to answer. I thought I'd have to leave a message. However, when he came on the line, I decided to grab the opportunity and talk while driving. I promised myself I'd be extra careful, observe speed limits and all that extraneous caution stuff.

"Found Rodney Bradford's murderer yet?" I said by way of a greeting as I pulled out of the restaurant parking lot.

"I can't discuss an ongoing investigation."

"I understand, but I'm involved in this investigation. I need to know what's going on."

"All the more reason I can't talk to you about it."

I honked when the SUV in front of me at the traffic light failed to realize that green meant *go*.

"Are you driving, Lindsay?"

"No." Technically, that was true. I was parked behind some moron who'd decided to take a nap. I honked again. "Have you considered the possibility that Lisa murdered Bradford after he told her about the money in my basement, and now Rick's blackmailing her?"

The driver in front of me finally woke up and blasted through the light that was already in the process of changing to red. I followed on his tail with the dispensation of being allowed to run a recently changed light when the idiot in front of you has been napping.

"I can't talk about an ongoing investigation."

"You sound like a broken recording. Can you at least confirm if Lisa has enough money to finance Bradford's purchase of my house?" Finally the jerk in front of me turned off onto a side street. I accelerated and prepared to make up for lost time. Cautiously, of course.

"I can't talk about an ongoing investigation."

A big, older model car pulled from a side street directly in front of me. I slammed on my brakes and cursed.

"Are you sure you're not driving?" Trent asked.

The vehicle that had pulled in front of me on the two-lane, winding, no-freaking-way-to-pass road had to be stuck in first gear judging from its speed. Amazing how all the jerks came out to play in the traffic at the same time I was getting ticked off at Trent.

"Yes, I'm driving, and I'm going to hang up now." No way was I going to share my information about the basement and the Murrays and all that when he wouldn't share any of his information with me.

I disconnected the call then leaned on my horn. The person in front of me continued to move at the speed of a snail on valium. The driver was so short, I couldn't see a head to even know if it was male or female. Could be the car was uninhabited. That would explain why the gas pedal wasn't being pressed.

I finally made it home without having a stroke and settled my Celica in the garage. One day I'd have to get it a home with straight walls. Good car like that deserved the best.

As I crossed my lawn to my porch, I admired the healthy greenery. I probably needed to mow it, but that would mean losing all the yellow and white flowers.

When I stepped onto my porch, I saw a piece of paper taped to my front door. Probably another ad for a lawn service.

I yanked it off and started to crumple it but then saw the words in large print: "NOTICE!" It was from the City of Pleasant Grove, signed by the mayor himself...or at least it was the mayor's signature stamp.

The city was not as enamored of my lawn as I was. In fact, they were threatening to fine me, condemn my place and send out a city employee to clean up my yard unless I did it myself within the next week, and did it to their satisfaction. How rude.

The notice referenced a "citizen complaint."

The house across the street was uninhabited. Paula wasn't bothered by my yard. When my lawn started keeping Fred awake nights, he either told me or sneaked over while I was at work and mowed it himself. At least, I assumed he did it himself. He could have some robotic mower that he guided from inside his house. I'd never actually seen him mow his own lawn which always remained the same length. I checked once to see if it was Astro-Turf. It wasn't.

There could be only one citizen who'd complain about my lawn. I remembered Rick's threat that things could get ugly if I didn't let him have my house.

I crumpled the notice. If forcing me to mow my lawn was the ugliest he could come up with, I had no worries. I'd do it as soon as I checked on Henry. Be a good way to work off pent-up frustration from the drive home.

I went inside and Henry trotted up to greet me. He wound around my legs, purred, bumped his head against my knee, then turned to lead me to the kitchen. I felt loved and needed—as long as Henry didn't figure out how to operate a can opener.

I came to an abrupt stop in the doorway to the kitchen. The room was a mess. Nuggets of cat food were scattered everywhere, some smashed, some intact. Water had splashed from Henry's no-tip bowl onto the floor. A chair lay on its side. A salt shaker had fallen to the floor. It wasn't broken but had spilled some salt.

I looked at Henry. He sat serenely beside his empty food bowl, blue eyes innocent.

"Did you do this?" Certainly he was physically capable of such destruction, but he'd always been such a well-mannered cat.

He lifted a paw, licked it and daintily rubbed his face.

I knelt to confront him eyeball to eyeball and saw that he was rubbing a scratch on his nose. "You have been up to something!" I scolded.

He gave me an indignant look and turned again to his food bowl.

On the side of his head I saw a red spot. I lifted the paw he'd just licked. A faint red stain marred the white fur.

As I looked more closely, I realized there were several small red spots amidst the cat food nuggets on my white vinyl.

I checked another paw.

More red.

My chest tightened. The thought that Henry could be hurt sent a burst of panic through me. I'd spent a lot of time trying to locate his previous owner and send him away when he first wandered up, but I'd since become attached to that arrogant, bossy feline and didn't want to lose him.

I held my breath as I ran my hands over his body, testing for sore spots, searching for wounds.

He purred then extricated himself and stared at his food bowl. Whatever catastrophic event had occurred, it was over, in the past, and he was hungry. Henry lives in the present moment.

He wasn't hurt.

The red spots hadn't come from him.

Slowly I rose from the floor and walked across the room.

The kitchen door opened when I turned the knob. Unlocked. I'd locked it last night after Fred left, and I hadn't opened that door since.

Someone had been in my house. Again.

But this time Henry had been there and, judging from the evidence, left his mark on the intruder. Four paws, four half inch claws per paw, and one mouth with half-inch, needle-sharp incisors.

Make that, *marks*, plural.

I smiled. Was this more of Rick's promised *ugliness*? Henry would have been thrilled to have the excuse to take a few chunks out of Rick's hide.

On the other hand, what if it wasn't Rick?

My smile went away.

I should call the police, report an intruder.

That meant I'd have to share my information with Trent even though he refused to share his with me.

But if we found Rick with scratches on his face and arms…my smile returned and I picked up the phone.

# Chapter Nine

The Pleasant Grove cops came and went, leaving me more than enough time to mow my lawn, trim my shrubs, water, fertilize and plant a few rose bushes, all before the lightning bugs came out to play. The cops did not find my crime scene interesting.

I'd called Trent, and he'd come over while the other cops were there. He remained standing in my kitchen after they left. "Lindsay, I'm sorry. I believe somebody broke in, but there's just not enough physical evidence to make a case."

He wasn't making any brownie points with me. And to think, I'd brought cookies to the man only two days before. "Not enough physical evidence? Really?" I flung my arms out in an all-encompassing gesture. "There's blood everywhere, including under Henry's nails! Why can't they work up a DNA profile?"

"And do what with it? There are no signs of forced entry—"

"My door was unlocked when I came home."

"I believe you when you say you locked it, but we can't prove it. You have an unlocked door with no sign of forced entry, cat food everywhere, specks of blood on your floor and on your cat that may or may not be his blood, and nothing missing."

"Nothing missing, thanks to Henry. At least go talk to Rick, see if he has scratches."

He folded his arms. "You do not want me talking to your estranged husband."

That was true. "Send somebody."

"I don't have any evidence to justify sending somebody. Anyway, I'm not even supposed to be here. I'm in homicide, not cat fights."

"You don't believe me."

He tried to take my hand.

I pulled away.

"I do believe you," he said, his expression entreating me to trust him. "And because I believe you, I don't want you staying here by yourself until after we get you some stronger locks. I plan to either spend the night on your sofa or you can come to my house."

I glared at him. "Really? Do I look like a helpless female who needs a bodyguard?"

Trent lifted his hands in a gesture of surrender. "Definitely not. I'd just like to be around to take a chunk of anybody who'd try to hurt you. Henry's had his chance, now it's mine."

"Hmmph!" I turned my back to him, but I was a little mollified and he knew it.

He put his arms around me from behind and kissed the back of my neck. "What good is it to have a macho cop in your life if you won't let him be macho once in a while and at least think he's taking care of you?"

I sighed, turned in his arms and gave him a proper kiss.

"The first time you spend the night with me, it is not going to be on my sofa," I said. "Go home. I need to mow my lawn. I got a notice from the City of Pleasant Grove. They're going to condemn my place if I don't."

He scowled. "Seriously?"

"Yes, seriously. I'm sure it was Rick. He knows the mayor and all those people. But my lawn does need to be mowed, so I'm not going to fight it."

"How about I mow while you put on your best frilly apron and whip up a spectacular seven course meal for dinner?"

I grinned. "How about ragged cutoffs, a frozen pizza and something chocolate for dessert?"

"Deal. Where's your mower?" He released me and moved toward the front of the house.

"In the garage. Lift up on the handle and tug the door slightly to the left."

"Got it."

"But then you're going home."

He turned back. "And just what are you going to do if somebody breaks in again?"

"I have safety chains on both doors. I'll leave them on, and if somebody comes in, they'll have to break the door down and make a lot of noise. That'll wake me up."

"And?"

I shrugged. "And I'll call you then go downstairs and pull Henry off the burglar before he does permanent damage to the intruder."

He stood there for a minute looking at me, the green in his dark eyes bursting out in flames. I could almost hear the sound of his teeth grinding. "We'll talk about it later." He turned and walked out of the house.

I admire a man who won't admit he's beaten even when he clearly is.

I looked down to see Henry had moved up beside me and was also watching Trent. "You like him too, don't you? Your opinion matters. Come on, let's clean up the kitchen and get you some fresh food. Sorry, no catnip again tonight. You have to be alert. When this is over, you can go on a week-long bender."

I filled Henry's water and food bowls, and he chowed down while I cleaned the floor. As I swept under the edge of the stove, my broom brought out something shiny. I leaned over and picked it up. A gold hoop earring. Could be one of mine or one of Paula's...or Henry could have yanked it out of the intruder's ear. Blasted cops hadn't done a very good job of investigating or they'd have found it. I'd have to point that out to Trent.

I slid it into my jeans pocket to show him later.

We had a good time that evening, Henry, Trent and I. Henry mostly hung around and slept since he had to take guard duty that night. Trent and I ate, talked and made out, and then he left. Well, he left after we had a rip roaring argument. His pride wouldn't let him leave me alone without a fight, and I didn't disappoint him. Nevertheless, we parted on good terms. I got a really nice kiss at the door.

We had so much fun kissing and fighting, I forgot about the earring until I was undressing for bed and found it in my pocket.

I carried it to my dresser and opened the small jewelry box my mother had given me for my tenth birthday. A tiny ballerina popped up and twirled to the tinkling sounds of the Blue Danube Waltz. I suppose my mother thought the gift would inspire me to be like that dainty, graceful ballerina even though I'd already been kicked out of ballet, tap, and jazz classes on the dual grounds of no talent and no interest. But my mother's never been one to give up either.

I poked through my small collection of earrings. Mixed in with the real gold and silver, gifts from my family, were the junk pieces I'd acquired. I did have a pair of faux gold hoops, but they weren't the same as the one I'd found on the kitchen floor, and both of mine were present and accounted for.

I held the earring in my palm and studied it, trying to guess its secrets, where it had come from, who'd worn it into my house.

It was late, so I didn't call Paula to see if it belonged to her. I'd ask her tomorrow, but I'd never seen her wear hoop earrings.

I closed my hand over the piece of jewelry, clutching it and trying to get psychic vibrations from the person who'd last worn it.

I'm no better at being psychic than I am at dancing.

But I knew someone who was almost as good as a psychic. Fred should know about this latest development, and he would either be awake or would pretend he was.

"I assumed you'd call as soon as Trent left," he said by way of greeting. "Did you have another break-in?"

"How did you know that? Do you have my house bugged?"

"I saw the cop cars. You weren't making enough noise to justify a disturbance call, your cookies are great but not so great the police would come to your house for them, so it was a simple deduction."

I noticed he didn't answer my question about having my house bugged. Sometimes I think he has every house in the entire neighborhood bugged. Maybe the entire country.

"Yes, another break-in." I told him what had happened and about the earring I'd found.

"Interesting. So there's still something in your house that somebody wants, and that somebody may be a woman."

"Or a man and a woman, as in Rick and Lisa."

"Too bad the police wouldn't check the DNA."

"They took a couple of swabs, but Trent said they won't go to the trouble to process it. I already cleaned it up or you could come over and have a look at it."

"Why would I do that? I couldn't tell anything simply by looking at it."

"It was just a thought. I never know with you. I think we need to go visit the new lovers, see if either or both of them show signs of being in a cat fight."

"*We*, as in you and I?"

"I don't think Henry wants to go visit them. He doesn't like Rick, and I doubt he'll be fond of Lisa. Of course I mean you and me!"

"I never know with you," he mimicked. "Let me do some checking on Lisa, and I'll get back to you."

"Is that a yes?"

"It's a *maybe*."

"I'll go by myself, and you'll miss all the fun," I threatened. He'd already hung up, but I knew he was hooked. If there's one thing Fred can't stand...well, actually, there are a lot of things Fred can't stand...but high on that list is not knowing the answer to a puzzle.

# Chapter Ten

Paula had seen the cops at my house too. "I was going to come over and check on you," she said as we prepared for the breakfast crowd the next morning, "but when I saw Trent was still there after the others left, I knew you'd be all right. I was hoping he'd spend the night."

I threw up my hands, accidentally knocking over my measuring cup and sending cocoa flying around the room. "Does everybody know everything I do and who I do it with? It's a good thing I'm not a secretive person."

"Yes, it is," Paula agreed then returned to her task of grating potatoes for hash browns.

As I cleaned up the cocoa, I repeated the details of my evening including my irritation with the cops for not taking the break-in seriously.

"My offer still stands for you to stay at my place until this is over," she said.

"I appreciate it, but I don't think anybody's going to come back for a second battle with Henry. Oh, that reminds me. Did you lose a gold hoop earring?"

She turned to me. "No, I don't have any hoop earrings. Why?"

We looked at each other in the bright light that reflected off the shiny surfaces of stainless steel ovens, refrigerators, pans and bowls. Through the one window I could feel the darkness from outside pressing against the sturdy walls, trying to seep in and take over the brightness. I wiped my hands on a paper towel and pulled the earring from my pocket.

Paula walked over slowly to get a better look at it. She peered down at the object in my palm then back up to me. "A stranger wearing this came into your house."

I nodded.

"That's disturbing."

And suddenly, knowing with absolute certainty that this piece of metal had been yanked from an intruder's ear, it felt very disturbing.

"Are you coming to my house tonight?" she asked.

A part of me wanted to say *yes*. The thought of spending the night in my house where strangers felt free to come and go and dig in my basement and fight with my cat and leave bits of jewelry sent shivers down my spine.

I shrugged in what I hoped was a casual manner. "It's Friday. When Trent gets off work, he'll be over with burgers. Maybe I'll let him stay the night."

"I don't believe you."

"I don't either."

We went back to our food preparation.

"You might want to keep a close eye on Henry when he goes outside," Paula said, her soft voice loud in the silence. "If someone wants in your house badly enough, they might decide to eliminate the vicious cat the same way they eliminated Rodney Bradford. I've never seen Henry turn down food of any sort."

Damn. We had to put an end to this thing soon. Following Henry on his nightly rounds to be sure he wasn't eating poisoned food was going to be quite a trick.

***

As soon as I got home and filled Henry's bowl I called Fred. "What did you find out about Lisa? Do you know where she lives? Can we go spy on her tonight after Trent leaves?"

"Have you ever heard of the word *patience*?"

"What is that? Some foreign language? Nope. Not in my vocabulary. Now about Lisa..."

"I found her. Lisa Bradford, formerly Lisa Whelan, also known as Brandy Fire."

"Brandy—what?"

"She's a stripper down at the Babes and More Lounge."

Suddenly I needed to sit. I pulled a chair back from my table. It was the one that had been on the floor last night. I didn't need to sit that bad. I returned it to its position and pulled out another one, then sank onto the hard wooden seat. "The new love of Rick's life is a stripper named Brandy Fire? Well, at least we know where she got her money."

"She doesn't have any money."

I felt as if my head was spinning like Linda Blair in *The Exorcist*. Rick was involved with a broke stripper? "What? No, wait a minute. If she doesn't have any money and Rodney Bradford didn't have any money, who was going to pay that exorbitant price for my house?"

"I have no way of knowing the answer to that question at this point."

I sighed. "It was a rhetorical question. So when are we going to talk to Brandy?"

"Tomorrow afternoon at 4:00. I chose that time because Rick has an appointment to show real estate, so he'll be gone, and it's late enough Lisa should be awake by then."

"I'll put it on my calendar."

"We'll be going as talent scouts for a strip club in Las Vegas. Dress appropriately."

"Talent scouts for a strip club? For such a conservative person, you come up with some wild ideas."

"I considered telling her you were her future husband's estranged wife, but decided that might not get us in the door."

"You're being sarcastic." I hesitated. "Aren't you?"

"Yes, I am being sarcastic."

"Okay, fine, we're talent scouts. About dressing appropriately, my G-string's at the dry cleaners. Any other suggestions?"

"Your usual uniform of blue jeans and tee-shirts won't work. You need something flashy but sedate."

"Oh, well, that narrows it down. Can you be just a little more specific?"

"Certainly. Your black pants suit that you save for funerals, that shiny red blouse, gold or silver hoop earrings, those red spike heels you bought two weeks ago and red lipstick. And fluff out your hair. Don't put it in a ponytail."

"What about underwear?" I asked. "You left that out."

"Unless you're planning to strip, it doesn't matter what your underwear looks like." He hung up.

Henry trotted to the back door and stretched up, reaching for the knob. He probably wasn't going to like it when I insisted on going with him. How embarrassing for a macho cat to have his mother tag along on his nightly rounds.

He strolled around the yard for a few minutes and didn't seem to notice or care that I was following. But then he darted across the alley and into somebody else's yard. I ran after him and tackled him.

For the first time, Henry and I had harsh words.

He growled.

"I'm doing this for your own good," I told him.

He snarled and tried to get away from me. I'd never liked it when one of my parents said those words to me, either.

I picked him up and carried him out to the front sidewalk then put him down. "Don't do that again. It's one thing for a cat to run across other people's property, but quite another for a chocolatier to do it. Let's just have a nice walk along this designated city easement."

He glared up at me and charged across the street, heading for the vacant house.

I charged after him and caught him just before he slid through the bushes and into that yard.

I wasn't sure what I'd do if he decided to attack me the way he'd apparently done the intruder, but I was sure I wasn't going to let him get away and be exposed to possible poison. He squirmed and flailed and made some ugly sounds that probably translated into feline swear words, but he didn't bite or claw me.

"I am so sorry," I told him as I picked him up and carried him back home. "You can't go out tonight, but I will open a fresh can of tuna."

I won't repeat what he said, but I'm pretty sure it wasn't even close to *Thank you* or *That sounds good, Mom.*

\*\*\*

It was dusk when Trent arrived bringing burgers and onion rings.

Henry hadn't stayed mad long, but he did make repeated attempts to escape. When I opened the door for Trent, I had to hold Henry back.

"Why can't he go outside?" Trent asked, handing me the deliciously scented bag and bending over to pet Henry.

"I'm protecting him." I explained Paula's reasoning and waited for the backlash I knew was coming.

Trent nodded and followed me to the kitchen. He was biding his time.

I got plates, silverware and Cokes for our feast, and we sat down at the table.

He waited until I had a big bite of burger in my mouth. "So you're protecting your cat from a murderer, but you don't think I should be protecting you?"

I chewed and glared.

"Don't you think that's being just a little hypocritical?" he continued, taking advantage of my temporary inability to argue. "Don't you think I care about you as much as you care about Henry? I was awake half the night worrying about you. If you insist on running me off tonight, I'm going to park in your driveway and stay there all night, and tomorrow I'll be sleepy and grumpy and my neck will hurt, and we're going to have a lousy Saturday date."

I swallowed. "Okay, fine, stay here tonight."

He set his burger in his plate and frowned.

"Hey!" I protested. "You just got your way. You're supposed to smile and be happy, not scowl at me." I bit into a juicy onion ring, savoring the onion flavor as well as the flavor of confusing Trent.

"I don't trust you," he said. "That was too easy."

I looked at Henry. He'd been lying over by the stove, pretending to doze, but the instant I looked at him, he shot up and went to the back door. "I'm doing it for Henry," I said.

Trent took a bite of burger, chewed and swallowed. "Okay."

"Aren't you going to ask me to explain?"

He shook his head. "Like you said, I got my way. I'm happy. I'm not sure I want to know the explanation."

I ignored him and explained anyway. "If you stay here, Henry doesn't have to be alert, and I can give him enough catnip to put him into a happy stupor so he'll quit worrying about not being able to go outside."

"I'm going to pretend you just said, *If you stay here, Trent, I'll feel safe and secure all night long.*"

I got up and put some catnip in a saucer then set it on the floor beside my chair.

Henry ceased his attempts to open the back door and trotted over with a happy meow.

"Watch this," I said to Trent.

That cat loves his 'nip. He began with a few dainty snorts then proceeded to lick at the bits of stems and leaves. Finally, inebriated enough to lose his dignity, he put his face in the saucer and rolled around.

"That is the funniest thing I've ever seen!" Trent said.

Henry gave him a slightly cross-eyed look, then lay down beside the saucer and purred softly. The entire event had taken less than fifteen minutes.

"I feel better," I said. "My cat's happily stoned, and, gosh, Trent, if you stay here, I'll feel safe and secure all night long."

He arched an eyebrow. "The first part sounded sincere."

My cell phone rang. Paula.

"Hi. You're just in time to join us for dessert. Bring Zach and—"

"I think your intruder just came to visit me."

# Chapter Eleven

We left Henry snoozing happily in his catnip-induced stupor and hurried to Paula's house.

"Are you all right?" I demanded as soon as she came to the door.

"I'm fine. Relax. It may be nothing. I may be overreacting."

"Not likely." Fred rose from the sofa as Paula closed and locked the door behind Trent and me.

"How did you get here before me?" I asked. "I live closer."

"I know the secret way," he said smugly, resuming his seat.

Paula smiled. "I called him first. I hated to bother you when Trent was visiting, but Fred insisted I should."

"Oh, good grief!" I sank onto the sofa beside Fred. "I can't believe you hesitated to call me. We weren't doing anything but eating and arguing."

Trent shrugged. "Yeah, it was one of our more exciting nights, but we don't mind being interrupted for a good reason." He walked over to Paula, took her arm and guided her to an armchair. "Tell me what happened." The quintessential cop.

Paula folded her hands in her lap. She appeared calm and collected, but I knew her well enough to know how good she was at faking it. "I'd just got Zach down for the night when someone knocked on the door."

Those folded hands in her lap were clenched pretty tight. I could see the white knuckles from across the room. I suppose when you think you've killed your abusive husband and hide from the cops for a couple of years, you learn to fear anybody who knocks on your door after dark. Or before dark, for that matter.

"I went to the door," she continued, "turned on the porch light and looked through the peep hole. It was a woman, but nobody I knew. I asked who she was. She said she was with Universal Insurance and wanted to talk to me about a key-man life insurance policy that Rick bought for you, Lindsay."

I shot to my feet. "What? Rick took out a policy on me? That proves it! He's trying to kill me so he can—" I stopped mid-rant. "Key-man insurance? That doesn't make any sense." I considered the ramifications of insurance often purchased on the life of an executive critical to the success of a company to insure the company could survive if something happened to that executive. "I don't understand. He wants to be certain the chocolate shop survives?"

"I don't think so," Paula said. "I think that woman was lying."

"Sit down, Lindsay." Fred patted the sofa beside him. "Let Paula talk. Remember that word we discussed earlier, *patience*?"

"And remember what I said about that word?"

"Go ahead, Paula. Tell us what happened." Trent crossed the room and sat on my other side, giving me a phony smile and lifting a finger to his lips.

Two of my three favorite men—the third was passed out at home—trying to keep me quiet.

Inadequate.

"She asked if she could come in, and I told her no. But I wanted to get a better look at her, see if she had any scratches, so I put the chain on the door and opened it a few inches."

I bit my tongue to keep from asking if the woman had scratches. *Patience*.

But Paula understood what I needed to know. Friendship means anticipating your friend's needs. "She was wearing a pant suit with long sleeves, so I couldn't see her arms or legs, and she had on a lot of makeup." Paula gave me a rueful smile. "Sorry."

"A lot of makeup?" I repeated. So much for *patience*. "Makeup like maybe a stripper would wear?"

"Well, yes, I suppose that's a good way to describe it. Her pantsuit was hot pink, she had really long, really black eyelashes, thick foundation, bright red lipstick, and Marilyn Monroe blond hair."

Trent gave me a curious look before returning his attention to Paula. "What did she say about the insurance policy?"

Paula spread her hands then clenched them again. "She said she just needed to ask me a few questions to verify what Rick put on his application. I told her to go ahead. I wanted to find out what she was up to. She asked if Lindsay was reliable, if she

114

showed up for work every day, what our hours were, pretty banal stuff, but then she asked if Lindsay had recently come into a large sum of money."

I didn't have to interrupt. She paused. I simply took the opportunity. "That's a strange question," I said.

"Not if that woman was the one who dug up your basement and found nothing where she thought she'd find money," Fred said. "You'd be her first suspect for having that money."

Paula nodded. "Exactly what I was thinking."

Trent whipped out his little notepad and pen. Good grief. He always carried those items, apparently even when he wasn't at work. If we ever made it to the bedroom, would he whip them out and take notes?

"This is not official," he said, pen poised, "but if you'll give me all the details you can, I'll see what I can find out about this woman. Did she give you a name?"

"Dorothy Wheeler. I doubt that's her real name."

"I doubt it too, but it could be a lead. Description, blond hair and lots of makeup. Tall? Short? Fat? Thin?"

"Taller than me. Probably Lindsay's height. Slim." She looked at me assessingly. "Very similar to Lindsay's build except—" She gestured vaguely in the area of her breasts.

"Similar to my build if I had a boob job," I finished for her.

Paula blushed. "A double, uh, job."

115

*Stripper*, I thought. *Lisa*. But I didn't voice my suspicions. Fred and I weren't planning to do anything illegal, but I felt it best not to share our plans with Trent. He can be really uptight about some things.

"Any other details you can remember? Jewelry? The way she walked? Accent when she talked? Kind of car she drove?"

"No jewelry, no accent. She drove a light sedan, white or beige. I'm sorry, I'm not good with car makes and models."

"No problem. This will help."

Paula smiled. She has a pixie face, and at that moment she looked downright impish. "There's one more thing. I got her license number."

Yay, Paula!

Trent scribbled in his notebook as Paula recited the number. Fred looked aloof and unconcerned, his normal expression. But I knew he'd remember the number and probably have a name before I went to sleep. Trent wouldn't get that information until tomorrow. He had to play by the rules.

\*\*\*

We played by the rules that night too. Trent slept on my sofa. He's about three inches longer than said sofa. I tried to get him to stay in my guest room, but he said he wanted to be downstairs so he'd hear if anybody tried to break in. He didn't think an intruder was likely to break in a window on the second floor where the guest room was located unless that intruder had wings, so staying up there would be pointless. He slept on the sofa, and Henry and I slept in my room.

Playing by the rules can be a crashing bore sometimes. Most times.

I slept late, until 6:00 since it was Saturday and we only serve brunch on Saturday. Henry slept late too, though he seemed none the worse for his binge the night before. Maybe I should switch to catnip instead of margaritas.

I tried to sneak quietly downstairs, but Trent sat bolt upright on the sofa when I hit a creaky step.

"Just me," I said. "I'm going to work."

He gave me a sleepy kiss and was snoring again before I got out the front door.

I was eager to get through the morning, close up the shop and go meet Lisa, check her for cat scratch marks.

I arrived home shortly after 3:00 and changed into my disguise. I took my hair down from the pony tail and spritzed it with water to bring out the frizz. The makeup took a little more effort, but when I finished and surveyed myself in my garage sale cheval floor mirror, I was pleased. The black suit, red blouse and big gold hoop earrings provided a nice contrast of somber and happy. A hooker going to her ex-husband's funeral.

I gave Henry some more catnip to placate him and stumbled over to Fred's in my four-inch heels. Those shoes were so tantalizing when I bought them. Who knew they'd be so much trouble to walk in?

With his white hair slicked back, wearing a black pinstripe suit and dark purple shirt open halfway to his waist exposing white chest hairs that almost covered a gold chain, Fred looked like a pimp trying to look like a businessman or a businessman trying to look like a pimp.

"Interesting disguise," I said. "I suppose we're taking your car."

"Of course. I don't want my dead body to be found dressed like this."

"Don't want to upset your kids, eh?" I asked in my ongoing efforts to uncover Fred's secrets.

He stepped out onto the porch beside me and locked the door behind us. "From what I've seen on TV, I think kids might find this outfit cool."

Curses. Foiled again.

We made our way slowly—always hovering right at the speed limit—across town to a trailer park in an older area of Kansas City. Following the GPS chip in his brain, Fred drove to a dilapidated trailer with orange curtains over the small windows.

"This is where Lisa lives?" I asked. "Are you sure?"

Fred arched an eyebrow, didn't even bother to answer that.

We got out and walked across the hard-packed ground to the door. True, I'd never met Lisa, but this was not the home I'd pictured for the most recent love of Rick's life.

The woman who answered the door was tall and blond and certainly got her money's worth for her boob job. She could have been the woman at Paula's door, but she definitely had no scratches on her face or hands or arms or legs or shoulders or stomach or the top seventy-five percent of her boobs. As for her butt, I couldn't say. Thank goodness. Her gold spandex shorts and top covered the essentials. Barely.

"Lisa Whelan? We spoke on the phone. I'm Dorian Gadeken, and this is Crystal McAlerney."

"Come in," she invited in a little-girl voice, giving Fred a huge smile. I'd had a tiny concern that she might identify me as Rick's ex-wife from a picture or description, but I needn't have worried. She didn't even look in my direction. Darn! All that effort with the makeup wasted.

Her living room was tiny and cramped and not overly clean. The gold shag carpet had several dark stains. Through a door on one side, I could see a small kitchen with dirty dishes piled everywhere, and through a door on the other side, I saw clothes on the bed and on the floor. The living room had probably held some of the litter of each room before she tidied it in anticipation of our visit.

When she invited us to sit, I could see Fastidious Fred weighing his options...stand the whole time and torture his cranky knees or sit on the stained green sofa and have to throw away those pants afterward.

He sat, and so did I.

Lisa perched on the matching arm chair, stretching her long, muscular legs in front of her, pointing her crimson-tipped toes in gold spiked-heel sandals toward Fred. He looked distinctly uncomfortable, and she smiled, unaware it was her dirty sofa making him uncomfortable, not her feminine charms.

"Ms. Whelan—" he began.

"Please call me Brandy." She crossed her ankles, ran her fingers through her blond curls and batted her eyes. I have nothing against false eyelashes. In fact, as a red-head, I think they can be a definite asset when nature doesn't provide enough of the real thing. But when they're so long and thick that a couple of spiders could be hiding in them, that might be too much of a good thing.

Okay, maybe I'm being a little extra tacky because the woman actually was gorgeous. Even with my bright lipstick and hot red shoes, I felt dowdy and plain sitting there in that frumpy living room next to that spandex-encased, overly-made-up, top heavy stripper.

"Brandy," Fred continued, "as I mentioned when we spoke on the phone, Crystal and I represent an entertainment company based in Las Vegas. We have agents constantly scouting for the best talent out there, and we'd like to discuss your career."

Lisa beamed and batted those eyelashes again.

"I heard there's a new hurricane forming down on the coast, stirred up by winds way up here in Kansas City," I said making a snide reference to her eyelash batting.

"Really?" She didn't sound particularly interested.

Fred glared at me. "No, not really. Brandy, if you're chosen, would you be interested in moving to Las Vegas?"

"Yes! I've worked Vegas before. I love it out there."

"So you have no ties to this area?"

She shook her head. "No ties. Kansas City is…" She looked around the room. "Kansas City isn't a very exciting town for a woman like me."

Definitely not planning to marry Rick and raise a family in my house. I'd be willing to bet Rick knew that.

"I understand you're recently widowed," Fred aka Dorian said.

Lisa flinched. Her sexy blond bimbo persona flickered, and for an instant I thought we might see a real person, but she got the mask back in place immediately. She dropped her gaze demurely. "Yes. I lost my husband a few days ago."

"Murdered." Fred dropped the word like a bomb in the small room.

She lifted her heavily lashed blue eyes. "That's what they're saying."

"We require that all our dancers have a spotless reputation with no hint of scandal."

"I'm not a suspect." She seemed genuinely indignant.

"We know that. But we also know Rodney was in prison when you met him."

Really? *We* knew that? Perhaps Fred and his invisible friends knew that, but it was the first I'd heard of it.

Lisa hesitated for a couple of heartbeats, and that time I saw an instant of a real person…a cold, calculating person. Only for an instant. She was good at her routine. "Rodney was a kind, gentle man. He made some mistakes, but don't we all? He cleaned up his act. We were going to have a life together."

"Yes, I believe you were even trying to buy a house."

She swallowed and lifted a hand to her hair, but this time the gesture was nervous rather than sexy. "We wanted to have a family."

"And live in his grandparents' old house?"

She licked her lips. A few minutes ago, the movement would have been sexy, but that image was slipping a little more with each of Fred's questions. "Yes. He was very sentimental." Her little-girl voice had dropped a couple of octaves.

Fred looked at her silently for a few long moments. She was starting to sweat. I could see it from across the room. I'd always thought Trent was good at getting people to confess, but Fred definitely had a talent for this. I fully expected Lisa to jump up and begin confessing to every crime from Rodney's murder to Jack the Ripper's murders.

Fred smiled, and she relaxed. "Why was he sentimental about the house where George Murray's grandparents lived?"

Lisa shot to her feet. She didn't teeter in her four-inch heels. Impressive. "Who are you?" she demanded. "Are you with the cops?"

"I'm sorry." Fred's expression was again guileless. "I didn't mean to upset you. You're a very talented dancer, but we have to check everyone's background carefully."

That seemed to mollify her, and she sat down again though she looked uncomfortable, and I didn't think it was because of the stains on her chair.

"So you didn't know Rodney was lying to you about his grandparents owning the house he wanted to buy?"

She sat stiffly erect on the chair. "Of course I didn't know he was lying. Rodney was my husband. I trusted him."

It was obvious even to me that she was lying.

"I understand." Fred rose, and I followed his action, standing beside him. He took a business card from his jacket pocket. "I think we have all the information we need. We'll be in touch. If you have any questions, please call me." He extended the card toward Lisa. She stood, now almost as shaky on her four-inchers as I was on mine. She made no effort to take the card. Fred laid it on her coffee table beside a stack of magazines.

He gestured for me to go ahead of him to the door, then he turned back to Lisa. "Who do you think killed your husband?"

She lifted her hands, fingers balled into fists, and for a moment I thought she was going to hit Fred. Instead, she crossed her arms over her bare stomach in a protective gesture. "I don't think I want to work for you. You ask too many questions. You need to leave."

We did.

Fred carefully dusted off his pants before he sat in his car.

Lisa stood in the doorway watching us.

"She met Rodney Bradford while he was in prison?" I said as soon as we pulled away from her trailer and out of her sight. "How did you learn that?"

Fred shrugged. "They got married as soon as he was released. It was an educated guess."

Fred doesn't make unsubstantiated guesses, educated or otherwise. "Okay, so it was a lucky guess. What does it mean?"

He pulled onto the street, leaving the dismal, grungy trailer park behind, and I gave a sigh of relief. "It means one of two things," he said. "Either she's one of those women who are attracted to criminals, or she targeted Bradford specifically for some reason. I believe it's the second, and I believe it has something to do with your house."

"Oh, goody! That makes me feel so much better!" I scowled at him. He didn't notice. He was completely focused on the road.

"There's a possibility she targeted him because she thought he really was the grandson of the previous owner, but that doesn't make sense. However, we need to consider the possibility that she used Bradford in some manner, and now she's using Rick."

I brightened at that prospect. "So she may kill Rick too?"

Fred eased the car around a corner. "She didn't kill Bradford."

"Damn."

"But I think she knows who did."

I twisted in the seat and turned toward him. "Then why didn't you grill her some more?"

"You have to know when an effort is a lost cause and it's time to switch tactics."

"You mean we can't beat her with a rubber hose?"

"No. Sorry."

I leaned back in the seat and gazed at the road ahead. The scenery was gliding slowly by. "Then what can we do?"

"I have some ideas."

I turned my attention back to his profile. Serene, unruffled. "Like what?"

"I'll let you know when I have something definite."

"Did you run those plates on the car at Paula's?" I asked. "Was that Lisa's car?"

"I don't know yet. I've been busy."

"Doing what?"

He didn't answer. I didn't expect him to.

# Chapter Twelve

Trent was waiting on my front porch when I got home. He rose from the swing as I approached, his eyes and his mouth both getting wider with every step I took toward him. "You look…uh…different. Nice. Interesting. Unusual. Why are you dressed like that?"

I tried to twirl enticingly but ended up on my butt. Damned four inch heels. I had to give Lisa credit for dancing in those things when I could barely walk in them.

Trent charged down the steps to help me up. "You okay?"

"Embarrassed but unhurt. My fall would have been softer if Rick hadn't made us mow my greenery."

He brushed the grass off my butt and grinned. "I'm glad you're not hurt, and I don't believe you're embarrassed. I've never seen you embarrassed. Is that what you plan to wear to dinner tonight? Should I go home and change?" He had on faded blue jeans and a denim jacket. It was much too hot for a jacket, but he didn't like to go anywhere without a gun, and people tend to freak out if they see the gun so he wears a jacket most of the time.

"No," I assured him. "I'm going to put on jeans. Just give me a few minutes. Would you take Henry for a walk? Don't let him escape or eat anything strange."

He continued to hold my arm, preventing me from leaving. "I realize this is probably none of my business, and I'm pretty sure I don't want to know the answer, but I have to ask. What were you and Fred doing this afternoon that you dressed up like this? The most dressed up I've ever seen you is when you wear your jeans with rhinestones on the butt."

I looked directly into those compelling hazel eyes and tried to think of an acceptable story that wouldn't be a total lie. "Visiting someone," I finally said.

His cop-gaze narrowed. "Who?"

A few more moments of eye-to-eye contact. I gave up. "You're right. It's none of your business, and you really don't want to know."

"I'll find out eventually."

"I know."

He released my arm. I went upstairs and changed into jeans and comfortable shoes then tamed my hair but decided to leave the makeup. He had included *nice* among the things he said about my appearance. I went downstairs and found Trent and Henry battling in the back yard. Trent was frazzled, and Henry was angry.

"Has he pottied?" I asked.

"Yes," Trent snarled, darting around to head off Henry's attempt to escape. Henry bared his teeth and hissed.

"Then put him inside and I'll give him catnip. If you don't solve this case soon, my cat's going to have to go to rehab when it's all over."

"You put him inside. I'm not getting anywhere near those teeth and claws."

"Oh, for crying out loud. He's just a big baby." I strode over to my hissing, snarling cat and picked him up. He glared at me and made some threatening noises but allowed me to take him inside. When I gave him catnip, he purred and twined around my legs.

Trent and I went out for barbecue, rented a movie and headed home. Henry roused himself to greet us, purring, his eyes still slightly crossed. Someday I was going to have to try some of that catnip.

Trent discarded his jacket and we cuddled on the sofa while we watched the movie.

"I'm not sleeping on this thing again tonight," Trent announced when the credits were rolling.

"Fine. I'm perfectly capable of taking care of myself. You go home and get a good night's sleep."

He shook his head. "I'm not leaving. I'm just not sleeping on this sofa again."

I thought about that for a minute. Well, actually it was probably more like a millisecond. "Okay." If we waited for my divorce to be final, we might both be too old to do anything, and my almost-ex had broken every marriage vow he'd made. Surely that was adequate nullification of the contract between us even without the judge's signature. I wrapped my arms around Trent and gave him a long, inviting kiss.

Sometime later, he drew back, breathing hard, his eyes slightly crossed even though he hadn't had any catnip. "Wow. What I actually meant was that I brought an air mattress."

"Oh." My fantasies came crashing down. "I think I need another Coke."

"Bring me a couple."

So we were back to the blasted guard-Lindsay-from-the-intruder thing. I was getting really tired of having that control my life, of feeling threatened in my own home, and Henry was really tired of not being allowed to roam his own territory.

I got two sodas from the kitchen, handed one to Trent and popped the top on mine. What a beautiful sound.

"Did you find out who owns that car that came to Paula's house last night?" I sat beside him and took a long, calming drink of cold, fizzy Coke. Next to chocolate, it's the best thing out there for stress relief.

"Yes, I found out."

"Who? Is it Lisa?"

"You know I can't tell you that."

"Yeah, you could. Maybe you won't, but you absolutely could."

He pulled me close, gazed deeply into my eyes and I thought maybe he was going to forget about the air mattress. He gave me a soft, sensuous kiss. "You tell me what you and Fred were up to this afternoon, and maybe I'll tell you who owns that car," he whispered intimately.

I pulled away. "No deal." I'd find out about the license plates from Fred eventually.

He sighed and leaned back on the sofa. "Let me make a guess about your afternoon's activities. It had something to do with Lisa. You must have checked on her and found out she's a stripper or you wouldn't have asked Paula that question last night about her visitor wearing the kind of makeup a stripper would wear."

"Quit doing your cop thing," I protested and kissed him again in an effort to distract him.

The doorbell rang followed immediately by a pounding on the front door.

We jerked apart. I have to admit, my heart was racing and not just from the kiss. Trent picked up his jacket and took out his gun then nodded to me to answer the door.

I looked out the peephole and turned back to Trent. "It's just Rick. Ignore him. He'll go away eventually."

"Open this door, Lindsay, or I'm calling the cops! Oh, I forgot, you have one of them in there with you already. Does he know what you did? Trent! Did you know my wife's been harassing my fiancé?"

That blabbermouth bimbo had obviously spilled her guts.

I burst out laughing. "Rick, do you have any idea how ridiculous that question is? How can you have a wife and a fiancé at the same time? Go away!"

Trent stood and tucked his gun behind him in the waistband of his jeans. "Let him in, Lindsay. We'll see what he has to say and then I'll get rid of him for you."

"Planning to shoot him?" I asked hopefully. A well-aimed shot could stop Rick from revealing my afternoon's adventure.

He lifted an eyebrow. I shrugged, gave up and flung the door open. "Rick, how nice to see you, though I don't remember inviting you. Did you bring your fiancé? I can't wait to meet her."

He was already standing inside the screen door, and he immediately charged past me and into my house. His blond hair was immaculate as were his gray slacks and long-sleeved white cotton shirt, but his eyes were wild and his face was red. "What the hell were you and Fred doing? And don't try to tell me it wasn't you! Lisa saw Fred's car, and she described the two of you! *A tall man with white hair and a tall woman with frizzy red hair.* You are so busted!"

I thought about trying to look innocent, but that would have been a futile effort.

"Hello, Rick." Trent moved up beside me and slid his arm around my waist.

Rick didn't even look in his direction, just kept his gaze focused on me. "I know you're here, Trent. I saw your car outside. You stay out of this. This is between my wife and me."

"Oh, stop it! Calling me your wife just because of a legality is like saying speeding is wrong because of a legality."

Trent moved up between Rick and me. "I don't think you should talk that way to Lindsay."

"I don't care what you think!" Rick made an effort to shove Trent aside. Have I mentioned Rick's

131

not the smartest man in the world? Trent grabbed his arm, twisted and put him on the floor in one second flat.

Usually I prefer to fight my own battles, but it was very satisfying to see Rick put in his place so easily.

"Police brutality!" Rick shouted. "I'm going to own you before this is over!"

"Right now, I'm not the police. I'm just a man protecting a woman from a threatening male. I'm going to release you, and then we're all going to sit down and have a rational conversation."

Trent stepped back, and Rick struggled to his feet, his face redder than ever. Not surprisingly, the incident hadn't calmed him.

Trent turned his back on Rick and walked over to the sofa. Rick's eyes got big and his face went from red to white when he saw the gun tucked in Trent's jeans. I'm sure that's why Trent did it. He was pretty cool even if he did steal my thunder.

Trent took a seat on the sofa, and I sat beside him. He flipped a hand toward my recliner on the other side of the room. "Please have a seat, Rick."

"I'd rather stand."

Trent smiled. "It's easier to talk when all parties are on the same level."

Rick glared at me then at Trent, but he sat.

"Lindsay, would you like to get our guest something to drink?" Trent asked.

"No."

"All right, then I guess we're ready to talk. Go ahead, Rick. I believe you had a question for Lindsay."

"I want to know why that b—"

Trent hadn't said a word to stop Rick. All he did was put a protective arm around me and reach behind him with the other hand.

Rick began again. "I want to know why Lindsay and Fred went to Lisa's place and told her they were talent scouts for somebody in Las Vegas."

I didn't look at Trent, but I could feel his muscles tensing. "Lindsay doesn't have to answer any of your questions."

But I'd be answering his questions when we got rid of Rick. Might as well get it over with now.

"I wanted to see if she had cat scratches."

"What?" Rick looked genuinely puzzled.

"Henry did some serious damage to whoever broke into my house the other night, and I wanted to see if it was her."

He paled, going from angry and puzzled to surprised and panicked. "Somebody broke in your house?"

"Two times. One time they dug up my basement floor." I watched him closely for his reaction to that.

He didn't disappoint me. His eyes flared and his lips moved as if he were speaking, but no words came out. He cleared his throat. "Dug up your basement floor? Did they find anything?"

"I don't think so since they came back a second time. At least, I assume it was the same person or persons both times."

133

"What made you think it was Lisa?"

"I found a gold earring."

He rose slowly from the chair and took a step toward the door. "No, Lisa didn't break into your house." His voice was thin and subdued.

I stood, sidling over to block his exit. Trent got up too and took my hand. Probably thought he could stop me from attacking Rick. "Yeah, I figured that out today," I said. "She'd have had to get scratches on just the lower half of her butt or right around her nipples. Henry wouldn't have been that careful."

As if he'd heard his name, Henry strolled in, looked at Rick, arched his back and hissed.

"Henry doesn't seem to like you, Rick. Maybe we need to see your arms. Maybe it was you and Lisa both in my house, but Henry only scratched you because he doesn't like you."

That brought back some of Rick's anger. "There's something wrong with that cat!" He moved closer to the door, farther from Henry.

"And maybe you were driving the car that brought Lisa to Paula's house last night." We hadn't talked about that incident, but I wanted to see how he'd react. I was pretty sure Paula's visitor was Lisa.

He stopped, looking confused. "Somebody broke into Paula's house too?"

"It's getting late," Trent said. "You probably need to leave now."

Rick glared at Trent and seemed to be deciding if he ought to protest. Henry moved closer and growled. "Keep that damned cat away from me. He's crazy."

Safer to take his anger out on the cat than on the cop. He turned and grabbed the door knob.

I reached down and picked up Henry. "He's a good boy, aren't you?" I scratched under his chin, and he purred. I turned my attention to Rick. "If somebody had cut off your balls when you were six months old, you might be a good boy now too."

# Chapter Thirteen

"I'll make sure he leaves then I'll move my car around behind your garage so it won't scare off any would-be intruders," Trent said.

I nodded. That would give me a little more time before we had to talk about the Lisa incident.

As soon as he walked out the door, I set Henry on the recliner, picked up my cell phone and called Fred. "Did you run those license plates yet for that car at Paula's house?"

"Yes."

I gritted my teeth and fought the urge to lay down my cell, go next door and strangle Fred. "Do you want to share that information with me?"

"Are you going to bake brownies tomorrow?"

"Brownies? Sure. That's a good idea. Trent's spending the night. We could all get together and cook out. But stop distracting me! Trent's car door just slammed. He'll be back any minute. Tell me who owns that car. Is it Lisa?"

"George Murray."

Trent opened the front door and I hung up on Fred without saying good-bye, the same way he usually does to me.

"Who were you talking to?" Trent asked, setting a deflated air mattress on the floor and looking at my phone suspiciously.

"I was talking to Fred. We're having a cookout tomorrow, and I'm making brownies." Every word of that was true. I don't approve of lying. Well, except when circumstances justify it.

"Okay, that sounds good. So why did you look guilty when I walked in the door?"

"Did I? Or have you just been a cop so long, you think everybody looks guilty?"

He grinned. "I've been a cop so long, I think everybody *is* guilty. Help me get this thing spread out, and I'll plug it in and soon have a reasonably comfortable bed."

"Be careful you don't upset Henry tonight. One swipe of his claws on that mattress, and you'll be sleeping on the floor."

Henry lifted his head and smiled. Maybe not in the same way we smile, but it was definitely a cat smile.

*** 

I love entertaining friends. I think that's one reason my chocolate shop is so successful. I not only make the best chocolate in the world, I have a great time serving it to people and watching them enjoy it.

I made brownies on Sunday, Trent and Fred joined forces to grill hamburgers and hot dogs, Paula brought corn on the cob, and Zach played with Henry, delighting in the new game of keeping Henry within the confines of my back yard. Henry, being the well-mannered cat he is, refrained from snarling

137

or hissing at the kid, but I could tell he did not like the new game nearly as much as Zach did.

After we stuffed ourselves, we lounged on my back porch in the cool shade of my overgrown bushes and trees. Trent had a cold beer, Fred and I enjoyed a bottle of wine, Paula sipped lemonade and Zach guzzled whatever liquid we put in his sippy cup, convinced he was drinking the same things we were.

Fred lifted his crystal wine glass and drank from it. He refuses to "ruin good wine by putting it in a plastic cup" so he'd brought over a set of etched crystal. Says if we break a glass, he has more of that kind, that they're his everyday crystal. He'd never let me drink from his special one-of-a-kind wine glasses, anyway, since I'm so clumsy. Personally, I don't believe he has any one-of-a-kind wine glasses, but I never know for sure with Fred.

"I wish I could have been there to see Rick on the floor," he said. "You should have snapped a picture with your cell phone."

"Darn! I should have! Can we do it again?" I looked at Trent.

He smiled and had another drink of beer. "If the need arises."

I can take care of myself, but it was kind of nice to know I had somebody to fight for me instead of against me.

"Do you think it was Lisa who posed as the insurance lady?" Paula asked.

"Probably," I said. "She fits the description, but if it was, her cohort in crime didn't know about it until last night. That was one of the few times I've ever seen Rick really freaked out, not in control."

Zach charged over to me and held up his sippy cup. "More wine, Anlinny!" Sweat plastered his blond hair to his head, his hands were grimy, he had mustard on his shirt and grape juice stains on his mouth. He was totally adorable.

"You bet, Hot Shot." I walked over to the ice chest, lifted out a bottle of grape juice and filled his cup. "You're not driving tonight, are you?"

He giggled and raced away, short legs churning.

I poured myself another glass of wine as long as it was handy. The real stuff, not the grape juice. "I would have liked to have a bug on Rick's wall last night so I could have heard what he and Lisa talked about after our encounter."

"You mean you'd have liked to be a fly on the wall," Trent corrected.

Paula choked on her lemonade. I gave Fred a meaningful glance, and he returned a blank stare. He and Paula both knew I was hinting for Fred to use his special skills and bug Rick's house.

"Fly, bug, some kind of insect," I said for Trent's benefit. "You all know what I meant. Anyway, I think Rick either learned some things last night that he didn't know about his girlfriend, or he learned there's another player in this game of *Take Lindsay's House*. In either event, that would have been one interesting conversation. It's too bad we'll never know what was said."

"Would you hand me another beer?" Trent asked in a blatant change of subject maneuver.

I pulled a cold can from the ice and took it to him then plopped down in the chair beside him. "You know, if we were all to pool our knowledge, we'd be able to catch Bradford's killer a lot faster and make my house safe so nobody felt compelled to sleep on an air bed in my living room. And since I brought the subject up, you've got to work tomorrow. You need to deflate your bed and take it with you. This is getting ridiculous."

"She's right, Trent," Paula said. "Lindsay and Henry are going to stay at my house tonight."

"And leave the treasure in my house unguarded?" I shook my head. "I am not exactly helpless, and I have a ferocious attack cat."

At the moment my attack cat was teaching Zach how to leap at the lightning bugs that were starting to appear in the evening dusk.

"I'm staying at your house tonight," Fred announced, "whether or not you're there. You can stay with Paula and I'll guard the treasure."

I reached over and took Trent's hand. "Well, I guess that settles that. Unless you want to sleep with Fred, you need to go home tonight." If Fred spent the night, I'd have extra time to nag him about bugging Rick's house.

Trent studied Fred. The two men are about the same height, but Trent does all that cop stuff and has muscles like you'd see on the cover of a romance novel. He also has a fierce look about him, the kind of look that would make a criminal stop and think twice before taking him on. Fred, on the other hand, is lanky and has a dignified look that would only frighten someone about to use the wrong fork at dinner.

"Thanks for offering, Fred," Trent said, "but I don't mind staying with Lindsay again. She's so self-sufficient, I don't often have the chance to take care of her."

Trent had never seen Fred kick butt and take out a would-be murderer about to make me his next victim, and Fred denies that ever happened when I try to tell somebody. So I can understand why Trent might be a little dubious about trusting Fred to protect me. It was kind of amusing but kind of insulting too.

I let go of Trent's hand and rose. I'd intended to rise imperiously, but that's kind of hard to do from a lawn chair. Nevertheless, I stood and looked at the two of them. "That's enough. I do not need to be protected. I do not need either of you staying at my house tonight, but if anybody's going to, it's going to be Fred because the rest of us have to work tomorrow. And speaking of that, it's getting dark, so we need to call it a night."

"I work," Fred protested.

"Where's Zach?" Paula exclaimed, and suddenly she was on her feet, her voice laced with panic. She still hadn't completely recovered from the nightmare experience her ex put her and Zach through and was a little overly protective of her son.

"It's okay," I assured her. "Henry's gone too. He probably went around the house, and Zach's chasing him."

But I didn't feel as confident as I sounded. There was too much crazy stuff going on to feel okay with a little boy and a cat disappearing in the dark.

"I'll go down the alley," Trent said, pushing through the shrubbery in that direction.

"I'll go around the house this way, you two go that way." Fred headed to the left, and Paula and I went right.

A terrible scream ruptured the quiet night, a sound like a creature in the depths of the jungle preparing to take down his prey.

"Zach!" Paula shouted, running toward the front of the house so fast I couldn't keep up even with my longer legs.

"Mommy! Mommy! Mommy!" Zach raced into her arms, sobbing hysterically. "Bad man hurt Henry!"

"Henry!" Now it was my turn to panic. I raced around the corner of the house in time to see Henry chasing a figure in a long coat and hood down the sidewalk. Apparently my cat wasn't hurt too badly. "Henry! Stop!" I charged down the sidewalk, determined to save my cat and trip his intended victim to put them on the same level so Henry could get to him to claw his face off.

Fred appeared from the other direction, his long legs easily carrying him ahead of me.

But the running figure had a head start. He made it to the beige sedan that waited at the curb with the engine running, slid in and peeled away. Henry let out another jungle cat yowl but stopped at the curb. Good. Chasing dogs was one thing, but I didn't need him to start chasing cars. What would I do if he brought a few home and I had to pay insurance on them?

Fred ran into the street and looked after the sedan. Trent brought up the rear, swearing with a great deal of expertise. He had his gun drawn.

"Shoot out the tires!" I shouted.

"I can't do that!"

Freaking laws. *You can't drive too fast. You're not divorced until the judge says you are. You can't shoot out the tires of somebody who tried to hurt your almost-girlfriend's cat.* Who makes up these stupid laws?

Fred came back down the sidewalk, shaking his head. "Same license plates as the car at Paula's house. I couldn't tell if it was a man or a woman driving."

Henry stalked over, and I picked him up. "Good boy," I said. "Good attack cat." I could tell he was disappointed he hadn't been able to draw blood.

"It was her." Paula stood beside me, her son held tightly against her.

Zach pushed away from his mother, reached up and petted my cat. "Henry okay?"

"Henry's okay." I looked at Paula. "I agree. I think it was the woman with the big boobs, and she wore protective clothing because Henry got her when she broke in before. My money's on Lisa. She's the right height."

Trent moved up beside me. "I suspect you're correct about the clothing. Nobody wears a coat and hood in this heat just to keep warm." His gun had disappeared again. Slick. "But you said Lisa didn't have any scratches on her."

I shrugged. "Could be Rick was with her when they broke in, and Henry scratched him while she got away. Henry doesn't like Rick. You saw that last night." But I didn't really believe my own theory. Rick had been shocked when I told him about the break-in. I knew him well enough to know when he was lying. He did it so often, it wasn't hard to learn the signs. And I didn't think he'd been faking his surprise last night.

Fred strode over to the porch, and Trent followed.

"Here's how they've been getting into your house." Fred stared down at something metallic lying directly in front of the door.

"Lock picks," Trent said. "We're dealing with professionals." He took out his cell phone. "Time to call in the cops."

"Why? They won't do anything. *Nothing was taken, nothing was destroyed,*" I mimicked.

"They'll file another report. We'll have it on record." He punched a number into his phone.

"I'm going home now," Fred said, "but I'll be back when everybody's gone. I'm spending the night, and tomorrow we're searching your house from top to bottom. There's something valuable in there or these people wouldn't take such risks to get to it."

# Chapter Fourteen

The Pleasant Grove Police were, once more, less than helpful. They wrote up a report and took the lock pick things with them in an evidence bag. Maybe one day they'd check for fingerprints, but I doubted it.

Fred spent the night in my living room on Trent's air mattress which Trent graciously agreed to loan him. I think those two could be friends if they weren't both so secretive about everything. But I suppose an air mattress is as good a place as any for a friendship to start.

When I left for work, Fred was already up and making strange noises in my basement. I gave him *carte blanche* permission to go through everything. I figured by the time I got home, he'd have my house cleaned and all my spices in alphabetical order. I was hoping he'd find a few missing things like my favorite iron skillet and my purple tee-shirt with rhinestone butterflies.

The morning went well. I made Chocolate Mousse for lunch, served it with a dollop of whipped cream and a strawberry on top, and saw a lot of happy faces.

Paula and I were cleaning up and preparing to close for the day when Trent called.

"We've arrested someone for Rodney Bradford's murder," he said. "I wanted to let you know before you saw it on TV."

"Who? Lisa? Rick?"

"Diane Hartman."

"Who?" I'd never heard the name. "Are we talking about the same Rodney Bradford?"

"She's his old girlfriend. They were together before Rodney went to prison, and then he dumped her for Lisa."

"Oh. Well. So you caught her. That's great."

"You don't sound like you think it's great. You can let Henry roam again and won't have to worry about somebody breaking into your house."

"I do think it's great. I really do. It's just that, well, I've become sort of personally involved, and I guess I'm a little disappointed not to be involved in the final solution. You never even mentioned that woman before today. I had no idea she was being considered as a suspect." I felt a little betrayed.

"Lindsay, you know I can't tell you everything that goes on in an official investigation."

"I understand. No problem." I did understand on a rational level, but I still had a problem with it. Okay, I knew that was irrational. Didn't matter. I was miffed that Trent had been in my house and shared my chocolate and even kissed me but still kept secrets from me. "So this woman killed Bradford because she was upset with him for dumping her?"

"That's our take on it."

"What was she looking for in my house?"

"She denies being in your house."

"Well, of course she does. I suppose she denies killing Bradford too."

"Yes."

"So she didn't confess, but you have evidence to prove she's guilty?"

"Yes."

"Like cat scratches on her arms?"

"I can't tell you that."

That sounded like a *no* to me. "What does she look like?"

He hesitated.

"Oh, come on! I'll see her picture on TV on the evening news!"

"Medium height, dark hair, ample bosom."

"That doesn't sound like the tall, blond woman who came to Paula's house."

"Wearing a wig, it could be. Paula's short. If Diane was wearing heels, she'd seem tall to Paula."

"What would she be doing driving a car registered in George Murray's name?"

Silence for several heart beats. "How did you know about George Murray's car?"

I considered telling him Fred told me, get all the secrets out in the open. But it wasn't my place to divulge Fred's secrets. "Computer," I said, feeling certain that was how Fred got his information.

"You found that information on the Internet?"

"You can find anything on the Internet."

"License plate registrations are not public information."

"That all depends on your definition of *public*. I need to go. We're busy."

"Hmmm," he said.

"Good-bye," I said.

"What was that all about?" Paula asked as soon as I hung up.

"They arrested Rodney Bradford's old girlfriend for his murder." I gave the counter a final wipe and tossed the towel into the laundry hamper.

"Well, that's good. We won't have to worry anymore about people breaking into your house or trying to hurt Henry." She didn't look convinced. "What were you saying about George Murray's car?"

"That beige car that came to your house and that Henry chased away last night is registered to George Murray."

In the silent restaurant, surrounded by clean, empty tables and counter stools, we stood for a long moment looking at each other, our doubts so loud I could almost hear them.

"Surely they have some sort of evidence against this Diane Hartman," Paula finally said. "The police know what they're doing."

"You really believe that? You were married to a cop."

Paula nodded, her jaw firming. "Good point. We still need to be careful."

***

I returned home to find my house much tidier than when I left and loud noises coming from my attic. Henry darted down the stairs and made a big production of telling me about this latest interruption to his once-orderly life. I gave him tuna and promised catnip later. He grudgingly accepted.

I went up to the attic where Fred sat in the middle of the floor clutching a hammer and looking more disheveled than I'd ever seen him. For one thing, he was sweating. Who knew Fred could sweat? His hair was a mess, tousled, more gray than white from all the dust, and his face was streaked with grime. He didn't look happy.

"There is nothing...and I emphasize the word *nothing*...in this house that anyone would risk jail time to obtain."

I sat down beside him. It seemed the polite thing to do. "That's good, right?"

"It makes no sense," he said.

"Want to hear something else that doesn't make sense? The cops arrested Bradford's old girlfriend for his murder."

Fred's scowl deepened. "You're right. That doesn't make sense. Did she confess?"

"No, she denies everything. But Trent said they have evidence."

"I don't suppose Mr. Stone Face told you what that evidence is."

*Mr. Stone Face.* Good one. "Of course not. He can't tell me *everything that goes on in an official investigation.*"

Fred rose. "I'm going to go home and shower. I'll be back in two hours and we can eat leftovers from yesterday's cookout."

I stood and headed out of the dusty attic. "And we can talk about the evidence that Trent won't tell me about."

"Maybe."

"I have chocolate mousse."

"You always think you can bribe me with chocolate."

I preceded him down the stairs, smiling to myself. There was a reason I always thought I could bribe him with chocolate. It always worked.

"Did you find my iron skillet?" I asked.

"You have an iron skillet in the back of the top shelf of the third row of kitchen cabinets. Is that the one you're talking about?"

"Yes. Kitchen cabinet, huh? Who would have thought to look there?"

"Did you know you have six pairs of men's silk bikini briefs with the monogram RLK under your bed?"

"Yes. Those belonged to Rick. They were his favorites. They somehow got mixed up in my stuff when I moved out."

"Somehow?"

I paused halfway down the attic stairs and looked at him over my shoulder. "We all know how. Let it go."

He nodded. I turned and continued on to the second floor landing. "Is there a reason they're under your bed?" he asked.

"Henry likes to drag things under there for his den, and I thought he deserved expensive things."

"I also found a purple tee-shirt with rhinestone butterflies mixed in with those shorts."

"Ew! Guess I won't be wearing that shirt again, not after it's been in close proximity to Rick's underwear."

"They're all covered in cat hair."

"Good." Maybe one day I'd give Rick back a pair or two of his expensive shorts.

\*\*\*

Fred returned exactly two hours later, clean and looking more like his usual self. We had hamburgers and chocolate mousse, and Henry had catnip. Soon everyone was satiated, and at least one of us was in a suitable state to be pumped for information.

I popped open fresh Cokes for Fred and me, and we moved into the living room.

"What evidence do they have against Rodney's old girlfriend?" I asked as we both sank onto the sofa. I stretched out, putting my feet on my coffee table. It's my coffee table, so I'll put my feet on it if I like.

"She has an amoprine tree in her front yard, and it's loaded with berries."

I shrugged. "Maybe those trees aren't common around here, but I'm going to bet that's not the only one in the area."

"Probably the only one with a direct connection to the murder victim. Perhaps not damning evidence in itself, but they also received an anonymous tip that Bradford was at her house a couple of hours before he died."

"Anonymous tip? They trust a tip from somebody who won't even leave their name?"

"Enough to investigate, and a neighbor confirmed seeing Rodney's car in the driveway that morning."

I sat back and sipped my Coke, considering that information. "This puts a whole new light on things."

"Not really. Diane claims he arrived at her house that morning saying she'd texted him to come by, that she had something important to tell him. She says she didn't text him, that she doesn't own a cell phone. The text originated from one of those prepaid phones, so that doesn't prove anything one way or the other. He did go into her house for a while, and they had coffee together."

I turned to look directly at him. "Coffee? Are you using that as a euphemism for something else?"

Fred heaved a frustrated sigh. "No. Bradford loved coffee. They drank coffee together. She said they had a nice conversation, and he left to keep his appointment with his real estate agent. That would be Rick."

"*A nice conversation*? Not likely."

"I guess we'll never know. Bradford's in no condition to verify or deny what she says. Amoprine berries do have a bitter flavor similar to coffee, so she could have done it."

We sipped our sodas in silence for a little while.

Henry strolled in, eased onto the sofa beside me and went to sleep, snoring softly.

"Cat scratches?" I asked.

"No, thank you."

"I mean, did this Diane person have cat scratches on her?"

"No, but the police are not as convinced as you are that the murderer and your intruder are the same person or even that Henry left scratches on your intruder."

"Oh, really?" Trent was going to be in so much trouble when I got hold of him. He could have at least assured his buddies that I knew what I was talking about. "So I guess they're not concerned that Paula's visitor and my potential intruder were both driving a car registered to George Murray?"

"No, they're not."

I wiggled my bare toes, increasing the blood flow to my brain, considering what all that meant. "We need to find out who's paying the personal property taxes on that car. Not likely Murray since he's in prison. Could be his grandparents. I'll bet they know who has possession of it and who would be driving it. And to think, they seemed so innocent!"

"The records show that Murray's paying the taxes and getting the license plates renewed."

"Is that possible?"

"Possible but not likely. It'd be pretty easy for anybody to use his name to do all that. The government just wants money. They don't care who they get it from."

"I see." I chewed my bottom lip and thought for a minute. "Then I guess we need to talk to Murray."

"He's in prison."

"So? Inmates can have visitors. I see it on TV all the time."

Fred studied me for a long moment before he finally spoke. "Lin, I don't think you have a very good idea of what a prison is really like."

I set my empty Coke can on the coffee table and swung my legs to the floor. "I probably don't, but

I'm going to find out. I can go by myself, or you can go with me, but I'm going."

"Okay. He's in a local facility twenty minutes south of here. I'll see if I can schedule an appointment for us."

That was easy. Suspiciously easy. He was already planning an excursion or he'd never have given in without a fight.

"When?"

"I'll get back to you on that."

"How should I dress?"

He gave me a look that suggested I'd asked a stupid question. "It's not a formal event. I think your jeans will be fine."

"What will our names be?"

"You'll be Lindsay Powell, and I'll be Fred Sommers. Honestly, Lindsay, sometimes I worry about you."

"You mean we're not going to pretend to be private detectives or mob members or the Prize Patrol?"

"Of course not."

"Sounds a little boring, but I guess I'm in anyway."

# Chapter Fifteen

Knowing Rodney Bradford's old girlfriend was in custody did not help me sleep even a little bit better that night. I insisted Fred go home. After cleaning my house all day, he deserved a good night's rest. I slept with my cast iron skillet beside my bed. Henry was pretty much sobered up from his catnip bout, and I trusted his guard cat abilities. Nevertheless, I woke before the alarm and decided I might as well go in and get an early start on my chocolate creations.

I was still a little groggy as I drove through the pre-dawn darkness, but as soon as I pulled into my parking space in the alley behind Death by Chocolate, I came wide awake. Something was wrong. Light should not be coming through the kitchen window.

I sat in the car a moment trying to rationalize. Maybe, just maybe, after Trent's disturbing call about Diane Hartman's arrest, Paula and I had been so distracted we'd forgotten to turn off the light in the kitchen.

I did not believe that.

Heart climbing up into my throat, I flew out of my car and over to the door...which was unlocked. Something else that shouldn't be.

Could Paula and I have both forgotten to check the door?

Maybe.

Not likely, but anything was possible.

I sent up a silent prayer that we'd both suddenly, unaccountably, become forgetful and careless, then I flung open the door.

Fire!

Flames shot up from the stovetop to the ceiling.

I slammed the door closed. *Cut off the oxygen.* I remembered that advice from somewhere.

I yanked my cell phone from my pocket and, hands trembling so badly I could barely hit those stinking little numbers, called 911.

This could not be happening! Death by Chocolate was my dream, my home away from home, the place I'd struggled for years to establish. I loved this place. Besides that, it paid the bills.

The 911 operator said she'd have someone there immediately and requested I stay on the line.

"No!" I hung up.

I could not let my chocolate shop go up in flames without trying to do something.

I ran around to the front and went in that door. It was smoky, but the flames were confined to the kitchen. For the moment.

I grabbed a fire extinguisher off the wall and lugged it to the kitchen door. Taking a deep breath, I opened that door.

Smoke and heat rushed out, and I stumbled backward, dropping the extinguisher, clutching the edge of the counter to keep from falling.

I righted myself, grabbed the extinguisher and went back to the open door. Death by Chocolate and I were not going down without a fight. I couldn't see what I was doing, but I lifted the nozzle and began spraying.

Those damned fire extinguishers don't last very long. I was just pushing forward into the kitchen when the worthless hunk of metal sputtered and died.

I tossed it aside and ran to the ice machine behind the counter, grabbed a large bowl, filled it with ice and tossed it into the kitchen.

At that moment the back door burst open, and men in yellow and black uniforms rushed in. Probably the first time in my life I was happy to see a man in uniform. Usually they just want to write me traffic tickets.

My first impulse was to dash in and help, but I hadn't been very successful so far. I decided to go out and close the door, cut off that particular supply of oxygen to the fire.

I started out the front door with the intention of going around to the back again, but met more firefighters who asked me to get out of the way. Just that one time, I decided to comply with an order. I went outside to stand on the sidewalk and watch helplessly through the plate glass window.

Damn, I needed a Coke but the Cokes were all inside with the fire.

A car pulled up to the curb and Paula jumped out. "What's going on? Why is there a fire truck in our alley? Why do you have black streaks on your face?"

I ran to her and restrained her from going inside. "It's on fire!"

In the ghostly light from the street lamps, her face went even more ghostly. "Oh, no! What happened?"

I flung my hands through the air in helpless frustration. "I don't know! It's in the kitchen. I tried to put it out. We need to get a better fire extinguisher. That damned thing wouldn't put out a candle flame!"

Paula straightened, regaining her composure, and took my arm. She handles crises better than I do. She's had more experience. "It's going to be okay," she assured me. "The fire department's here. You have insurance. We can't do anything right now. Let's go sit in my car until it's over."

So rational.

"No! I'm going to pace up and down this sidewalk and worry. I can't sit quietly in your car and fiddle around while Death by Chocolate burns!"

"All right. I'll pace and worry with you." Paula's a good friend.

It seemed like we'd been pacing for an hour or two, but Paula said it was only a few minutes before a fireman came out holding his hat in his hands. I took that as a good sign, that he didn't need the head protection anymore.

"Did one of you call 911?"

"I did. Is the fire out?"

"Yes, ma'am. You've got one heck of a mess in there, but we got to it before much damage was done."

I burst into tears and hugged him.

He laughed and pushed me away. "I'm pretty dirty, ma'am."

I stepped back. "I don't care. Thank you so much for saving my place!"

"Glad we could help. You ladies need to be more careful in the future. The fire started in a pan of grease left on the stove with the burner on. If we'd been a few minutes later, the whole place could have burned down."

I looked at Paula. She looked at me.

"We did not leave a pan of grease on the stove," I said quietly.

"And we did not leave a burner turned on," Paula added.

"Yes, ma'am." He didn't believe us. "I need to get some information from you, and then we'll let you get back into your place so you can start the clean-up."

We gave him the information he needed for his report, and he gave us what we needed to file an insurance claim.

Finally they were all gone, and Paula and I went in to survey the damage.

It was definitely a mess. The kitchen walls were black, and the whole place smelled like smoke. The floor was covered in foam, probably mostly from my efforts with the fire extinguisher. I hadn't managed to get any of that goop on the stove where the fire had blazed. The sturdy equipment was coated in soot but basically undamaged. A large black pan sat on top of the stove. That pan had been bright stainless steel yesterday.

"This fire was deliberately set," Paula said. "We need to call the police."

"Yeah. They've been so helpful the other times I called them."

She went to the back door and locked it. "Let's go in the other room, sit down and discuss this."

I nodded. "I could use a Coke."

We got drinks then sat at a table close to the front door which we propped open to get some clean air.

I took a healthy swig of my soda. It burned and bubbled down my throat and helped clear out the taste of smoke. "The back door was unlocked when I got here."

Paula folded her hands on the tabletop. "Apparently our mysterious friend has another set of lock picks."

"And since Diane Hartman is in jail, I'm going to take a wild guess and say she didn't break in here and set that fire. Maybe she murdered Bradford, but I don't think she's the one who broke into my house or came to visit you, and I know she didn't do all this." I waved my hand around the smoky restaurant.

Paula nodded. "This adds a new angle. If somebody is trying to find something hidden in your house, why burn down your restaurant?"

I finished my Coke then got up from the table and went rummaging for leftover chocolate. I found a piece of cake, ate a couple of bites, and suddenly everything fell into place. Chocolate has a beneficial effect on the brain. "Rick did it!" I said.

Paula turned to look at me. "Rick's a jerk, but even he wouldn't burn down your restaurant."

I raised my eyebrows. "Are you so sure?" I moved back to the table with a fresh Coke for me and a slice of cake for Paula. "Think about it. He and Lisa want my house. If I lose my restaurant, I'll be more inclined to sell him the house to get the money to reopen this place."

She shook her head doubtfully. "I don't know. That may be reaching a little. I realize you have plenty of reasons to be angry at Rick, but you do tend to blame him for everything bad in your life." She held up a hand before I could protest. "Granted, he's responsible for ninety percent of the bad things in your life. But remember when you got three speeding tickets in the same day and you said it was Rick's fault?"

I glared at her. Friends weren't supposed to remember things like that. "It was his fault. He made me mad, and I wasn't watching carefully enough for cops."

She rolled her eyes, shoved back her chair and stood. "I'm going to get you some more chocolate, and we're going to call the police then make plans to get this place cleaned up so we can reopen."

"Fine, but think about this. Rick and his new girlfriend want my house. They want it bad. When I refused, he threatened me. *Don't fight me on this or things are going to get ugly*. It doesn't get much uglier than burning down my chocolate place."

Paula returned to the table with a cookie for me. She hadn't finished her Coke or her cake. Caffeine and chocolate deficit would explain why she wasn't thinking straight.

"The back door was unlocked when I got here," I said. "It's conceivable that mysterious woman has another set of lock picks, or maybe she didn't need them. I changed the locks on my house last fall after your psycho ex tried to poison me, so Lisa and Rick would have had to pick that lock to get in, but Rick still has the spare keys to this place. Maybe he just unlocked the door with his key, he and Lisa waltzed in, poured some grease in a pan, turned on the stove and left."

Paula drew in a deep breath, released it in a whoosh and sat back in her chair. "You know what? It actually is possible. We really need to call the police."

"You do that, for all the good it'll do." I pulled out my cell phone. "While you're doing that, I'm going to talk to Rick."

I had to call him twice. The first time, it went to voicemail, but the second time he finally woke up.

"Death by Chocolate is still standing. I came in early before the fire had a chance to do any real damage."

"Lindsay? What time is it? What are you talking about?"

"I'm talking about the fire you and poor little Lisa set in my restaurant. The police are here, and they said they've found fingerprints." Okay, I know I said I don't approve of lies, but lying to Rick doesn't count. It's on the same level as lying to the IRS.

Neither Rick nor the IRS is honest enough to deserve the truth.

"What are you talking about?" he repeated, but this time he was wide awake. I had his attention.

I hung up.

# Chapter Sixteen

Same old story. The cops came, the cops went. These cops did take me a little more seriously since the sidewalk in front of my restaurant was the scene of a murder only a few days before.

All morning I halfway expected Rick to come charging in, demanding to know what was going on, schmoozing with the cops, proclaiming his innocence. I guess that means I only half believed my own accusations of his guilt. When he didn't show up, I realized it actually was possible, even probable, that he did try to destroy my place. That thought made me a little sick to my stomach, but a can of Coke soon put that right.

It was noon by the time Paula and I got everything taken care of, including contacting a professional service to clean and repaint. They estimated they could have us back in business by the weekend. Since Saturday was our slowest day. I put a sign on the door saying we'd be closed until Monday.

Then I went straight to Fred's house.

He opened the door and frowned. "You look terrible. Why do you have soot all over you? Why do you smell like smoke? Did you burn some cookies?"

"Rick tried to burn down my shop." I pushed past him, heading across his hardwood floor toward his leather sofa. On those surfaces, anything I dribbled could be easily cleaned.

"Wait!" He produced a large white towel and threw it over the sofa. "Now you can sit. You're covered in soot."

I sank down onto the towel-covered sofa. "I know that. Stop obsessing about a little soot. We have bigger things to obsess about. Did you hear what I said?"

He sat in the matching recliner. "I heard you. I'm waiting for you to continue. Did you catch Rick in the act?"

"No." I told him why I thought Rick was guilty.

He nodded. "That's actually a very logical conclusion."

"You sound surprised."

"That Rick would try to burn down Death by Chocolate? No, that doesn't surprise me. He did threaten you, and the man has no scruples."

"No, you sound surprised that I came to a logical conclusion."

"You're not always logical when it comes to Rick."

I wiped a hand across my grimy forehead then held the grimy hand an inch above the immaculate forest green leather arm of Fred's sofa. "Take that back."

For a split second, he looked uncomfortable. But only for a split second. I might have imagined it. "Do you want to go visit George Murphy in prison?" he asked, successfully distracting me from any malicious activity I'd been contemplating.

"Yes."

"Go take a shower and meet me back here at four."

Fred has a way of winning arguments without ever raising his voice.

***

I showered, fed Henry and was so exhausted I took a short nap in spite of my cat's noisy demands to go out and prowl. I considered letting him roam for a while now that I was certain Rick and Lisa were the intruders. Rick wouldn't harm a defenseless cat. On the other hand, I would have never thought Rick would burn down a defenseless restaurant. After consideration, I decided Henry had to remain inside.

We needed to figure out what was going on with my house and put a stop to it soon before Henry called the ASPCA and reported me for cruelty.

I was at Fred's house by 4:00. He inspected me carefully before he let me sit in his white Mercedes.

"I showered," I told him through gritted teeth.

"You might have missed a spot."

I slid into his car and slammed the door.

Even with his speed-limit driving, we arrived at the small prison in less than twenty minutes. Creepy to think it was that close.

We stopped at a gate. Fred handed the guard something. The man looked, handed it back, pressed a button that opened the gate, and waved us on through.

"What did you give him?" I asked.

"Identification."

"What kind of identification."

166

"Valid identification."

"How did you manage to get us in as visitors on such short notice?"

"I asked the right person." He pulled into a parking spot.

I was going to be spending a lot of time at home the next few days, waiting for Death by Chocolate to be clean again. Maybe I could spy on Fred and learn some of his secrets.

"Are you coming with me or staying in the car?" he asked.

I put my spy plans on hold and got out.

We went through a couple more guards, signed in and were finally seated in a large room with half a dozen rectangular tables surrounded by chairs. A man and woman at one of the tables on the far side of the room leaned toward each other, talking quietly. Except for the armed guard standing beside the door, it was actually pretty mundane. No bars between tables or men in stripes sitting around whittling with homemade shivs.

Fred and I sat on one side of a table in the middle of the room.

"Don't we have to talk on phones through thick glass?"

"You watch too much television. George Murray was convicted of dealing drugs, not being a serial killer."

A door whooshed open, and I turned to see a man in a blue shirt and blue work pants being escorted to our table by another guard. The man in blue wasn't wearing handcuffs or leg irons.

He sat down across from us then smiled up at his escort. "Thanks, Ed."

*Ed*? He was on a first name basis with the guard? Weren't guards and prisoners supposed to hate each other?

Ed nodded and moved away to stand beside the other guard.

Fred rose and extended a hand across the table. "Fred Sommers."

The prisoner shook Fred's hand. "George Murray." He stood about average height, had brown hair and brown eyes. Except for a tattoo of an angry eagle on one forearm and a tattoo of a heart with lopsided initials on the other, he looked quite ordinary.

"Lindsay Powell," I said. The words came out as kind of a croak, so I cleared my throat and tried again.

Suddenly he didn't look so ordinary anymore. Something shifted behind those dark eyes. He recognized my name.

"Lindsay lives in your grandparents' old house," Fred said.

"Yeah?" was Murray's only reply.

"There have been some odd occurrences in that house."

Murray grinned. "Odd? You mean like ghosts? Surely you folks don't believe in ghosts, do you?"

Fred straightened his glasses though they hadn't been crooked and returned Murray's smile. "More like flesh and blood people digging around in Lindsay's basement."

Murray's grin remained in place, but it looked strained as if his facial muscles were fighting to turn down instead of up.

I thought we'd come to talk about the beige car registered in his name, but this line of questioning was interesting. He definitely knew something about my basement.

"We talked to your grandparents," I said. "They mentioned you spent some time with them before you, uh, when you were younger."

"You talked to my grandparents?" His face softened, he folded his hands, and his gaze dropped to the table as if the tough guy didn't want us to see his tender side.

"You love your grandparents, don't you?" I asked, feeling a sudden rush of tenderness. Fred shot me a glare and kicked me under the table.

Murray lifted his gaze and glared at me too. "Course I do! Everybody loves their grandparents. What do you think, I'm some kind of a psycho?"

*Yes.* "No, of course not!"

"We thought you might have some idea of what those people were looking for in your grandparents' old basement." Fred resumed control of the questioning.

Murray shook his head. "How would I know?"

Fred shrugged. "Boys are curious. They explore hidden places that adults ignore. Perhaps you came across a secret bookcase with old books or a hidden room with an antique chest."

I turned my head slowly and looked at Fred. Where was Mr. Practical coming up with this fanciful stuff?

The corner of Murray's mouth twitched. "Nah. That's just an old house. Nothing special about it. I'm surprised it's still standing. Probably fall down around you one day."

I shifted on the hard, wooden chair. Now in addition to everything else, I'd be watching the ceiling for signs of collapse.

"It's a solidly built structure." Fred sounded intent on reassuring me. He probably didn't want me calling him in the middle of the night if a piece of ceiling molding came loose.

Murray lifted one shoulder in a half-hearted shrug. "Yeah, whatever. Look, I don't know anything about anybody breaking into your house. Sorry I couldn't help you." He started to rise, but Fred lifted a restraining hand, and Murray sat down again.

"Do you know why your former cellmate, Rodney Bradford, wanted to buy your grandparents' old house?"

There it was again, that darkness at the back of his eyes. He forcibly lifted the corners of his mouth in a makeshift smile. "Me and Rodney got close, talked a lot. You do that when you're in a place like this. I told him about my grandparents, how my visits with them were the best times of my life. I guess he just wanted to pretend they were his grandparents and he had all them good times."

Fred nodded. "I guess that makes sense. He married a woman he loved and thought they could have a good life together in that little house where other people had been happy."

The darkness got darker and the smile more forced. The corners of his mouth were actually turning white with the effort. "Exactly."

"He met Lisa while he was in prison. Did you know her?"

Murray gave up the effort. His face sagged into a scowl. "Why would I know her?"

"You and Bradford were cellmates. You were close, talked a lot. Surely he told you about the woman he loved."

Murray hesitated. "Yeah, sure, he told me."

"You didn't approve of his relationship with Lisa?"

"It don't matter whether I approved or not. None of my business who he married."

"She's going to end up living in your grandparents' house," I said.

He sat upright, suddenly intent. "What? Where'd she get the money to buy a house?"

"She doesn't need money. You see, I don't actually own the house outright. My estranged husband and I own it together, and he's offering me a really good deal in the divorce if I'll let him have the house. He and Lisa are getting married as soon as our divorce is final, and then she'll be living in your grandparents' old house where you had such good times when you were growing up." Lying for a good cause doesn't count, either.

Murray's hands clenched on the table, his knuckles white.

"I guess that's something you're gonna have to work out with your husband. Look, I got kitchen duty this week. I need to get back to work." He rose, and this time Fred stood with him. I remained seated. Fred wasn't finished with him yet.

"Of course. Just one more question. Your car, the beige Ford you owned when you were sent to prison, what happened to that car?"

Murray looked at Fred, then me, then the guard, then the wall on the right and the wall on the left. "My car?"

"Yes, your car, the beige Ford."

"I don't know. I might have left it with a friend. Or maybe it was in a garage being worked on. Could be my grandparents have it. Did you ask them?"

"No, we didn't."

"Then maybe you ought to ask them. I'm in the slammer. Some old car doesn't matter to me in here." He started toward the door. "Ed, I'm ready to go."

Fred grabbed his arm. "Thank you for talking to us." He forcibly shook Murray's hand again then held it for an extra beat, his gaze on the man's forearm.

Murray yanked his hand away, gave Fred a totally freaked-out look and practically ran for the exit.

"Okay," I said, rising to stand beside Fred, "what was that about? Why were you so interested in his tattoo?"

"The initials."

I shrugged. "They're ugly, like the artist was drunk when he did it."

"Or like a really bad tattoo artist, maybe a self-styled prison artist, tried to turn one set of initials into another."

# Chapter Seventeen

My cell phone rang as we were walking down the long hall that led out of the prison.

Trent.

"You had a fire at your restaurant this morning and you called the police to report it as arson, but then you, what? Forgot my number?" He didn't sound happy. Fine. See how he liked being left out of the loop the way he was always doing to me.

"You know I can't divulge information relating to an ongoing investigation," I replied.

He was silent for a moment, probably deciding whether to be mad at me or ignore me. He chose the latter. He usually does. "Where are you now?"

"In prison."

"What?"

"Just kidding. I'll be home in half an hour. Why?"

"I want to see you and make sure you're okay. You've had a bad morning. I really wish you'd called me."

"It was early. You were still asleep. You know what time I go in to work, and I went in even earlier this morning."

"Okay, fine, it doesn't matter. How about I stop by in a couple of hours and bring over a pizza or something?"

"That would be good. I'll be waiting." I disconnected and put my phone in my purse.

Fred and I pushed through the last door, outside into the sunshine. Prison might be less frightening and more mundane than I'd anticipated, but it sure did feel good to breathe free air again even if that air was about ninety-five degrees and muggy.

We settled in Fred's car and were soon cool and comfortable as we headed home, driving in the middle lane. Not too fast, not too slow. Well, way too slow for me.

"Murray doesn't seem to care for Lisa," I said.

"It's not like you to understate things, Lindsay. I thought the man was going to have a stroke when you told him Lisa would be living in your house."

I smiled. "That was a good one, wasn't it? I wonder if Lisa was dating…well, doing whatever you call the prison version of dating an inmate…with both of them."

"I think you're on the right track. The initials in that heart have been changed and not by a trained tattoo artist. The 'K' is lopsided and overly large, as if it might once have been an 'L' until somebody added two strokes below. The 'D' is fuzzy around the edges and has a really thick left side. Could have been a 'W' at one time."

I leaned back and considered that. "LW. Lisa Whelan. So you think Murray and Lisa had a prison romance thing going, Murray had her initials tattooed on his arm, and then Bradford stole her?"

"He knew enough about her to know she couldn't afford to buy your house."

"He did, didn't he?"

"But I think he knew her before he went to prison. While the heart tattoo is certainly not the work of someone like Ed Hardy—"

"Who?"

Fred rolled his eyes and sighed. "Let me rephrase. While the heart tattoo is not the work of an expert tattoo artist, it's the same quality as the eagle, and it's a lot more professional than the two changed initials. Based on that information, it's possible Murray and Lisa were together before Murray was convicted and sent to prison."

"I get it!" I turned to face him. "Murray was dating Lisa and told her where he hid drugs or whatever. Then Murray went to the slammer and became buddies with Bradford. He introduced his cellmate to his girlfriend, and the cellmate stole her then got out of prison before Murray, and the two of them tried to get Murray's grandparents' old house because Lisa knows that's where Murray hid whatever it was he hid."

"That theory brings us to another interesting question. Neither Bradford nor Lisa had any money. How did they plan to buy your house?" He never took his eyes from the road, not even for an instant, but I could feel his gaze on me. He probably did it using psychic waves. Or psychotic waves. Whatever.

I thought about it for a minute then groaned and sagged back against the seat as several more pieces of the puzzle fell into place. "Rick."

Fred nodded, his expression grim. "It's possible that your many accusations of Rick's malevolent intentions were justified."

I stared at the road ahead and let all the implications sink in. "Lisa and Bradford needed to get the house, so they made a deal to share whatever's in there with Rick, the current owner. One of the current owners. That is so—" I threw my hands into the air, unable to come up with a word horrible enough to describe such a scenario.

"I believe the word you're looking for is *possible*," Fred said. "Or perhaps *probable*."

"Not really." I sighed. "But unfortunately, it all fits. If there's money involved, Rick will be right there."

Fred was silent. He does that a lot, but this particular silence seemed very loud. He was waiting for me to continue, but I had nothing more to say on that subject.

Or did I? Rick struck some kind of a deal with Lisa and Bradford to help them take my house away from me and split the buried treasure three ways.

Only Bradford was dead, so now it would only be a two-way split. More for both of them.

I groaned again.

"Exactly," Fred said, breaking that shrieking silence. "Rick may be involved in Bradford's murder."

I dug around in my purse, hoping to find a chocolate bar or even a few crumbs from a brownie. The realization that I was once married to an arsonist/murderer was a pretty stressful event. "Do you think we could find a convenience store and get me a Coke?"

"Yes." He hit the accelerator, cut across two lanes of traffic and took the closest exit. For Fred, that was an expression of deepest sympathy.

***

I was so ready for Trent when he arrived later that evening with a pizza. Henry was on my heels and tried to dart out the door when I opened it. I shoved him back inside—Henry, not Trent—where he began pacing, yowling and pleading his case with Trent. I could have told him that was pointless with Mr. Stone Face. Very appropriate name Fred had given him.

As soon as Trent set the pizza box on the kitchen table, I threw myself into his arms. He held me for a few moments, patting and stroking and murmuring soothing words. It was quite lovely but necessarily brief. The pizza was getting cold.

I got plates and napkins while Trent opened a couple of Cokes, and we sat down to feast on a deep dish everything-but-the-kitchen-sink pizza.

I started talking as soon as I finished my first piece. I figured if Trent had his mouth full of pizza, it would be more difficult for him to interrupt with pointless questions such as "You what?" and "Are you nuts?" and "Why did you do that?"

Sure enough, I'd barely begun to tell him about our interrogation of Murray when he choked and sputtered and said, "You what? You went to prison? Why did you do that? Are you nuts?"

I ignored him and went on to tell him everything, explaining about Rick's perfidy and his and Lisa's involvement in arson and murder.

When I finished, he looked at me for a long moment, shook his head, went to the refrigerator and got another Coke. I wondered if I should talk to him about that. Wouldn't do for a cop to get addicted to Coke.

I ate another piece of pizza while he sipped his fresh soda and considered the new evidence Fred and I had uncovered.

Finally he leaned back from the table and regarded me intently. "Assuming you're right, where's the mysterious treasure Murray hid in this house? If Fred couldn't find it, I'd be willing to bet the farm it's not here."

"Yeah, Fred and I talked about that on our drive home. He says he doesn't like to make unsubstantiated guesses, but if he did something that rash, his guess would be that the first intruder found what he or she was looking for."

"Hmm. Did Fred make an unsubstantiated, rash guess as to who that first intruder might be?"

"Murray's new girlfriend, KD. Even as we speak, he's trying to figure out who KD might be. She got the goodies, but Lisa and Rick don't know that, and they're still trying to get my house, or get into my house, as the occasion may be. Remember

179

when Rick came over here, all upset because Fred and I had interviewed Lisa? He seemed surprised that somebody had broken into my house. My theory is that the second break-in was all Lisa's doing, that she's trying to get the treasure and then double cross Rick. Maybe she's planning to murder him like the two of them did to Bradford. That would solve a lot of problems."

"For you, not for her."

"Oh, well, yeah." I shrugged. "I guess I was thinking only of myself. You're right. If she kills Rick, she won't have the money to buy my house. It was just a pleasant thought. But you must admit, the rest makes sense."

"Not completely. You said Lisa had no cat scratches."

"I know. That's an unresolved issue, but everything else fits, including the possibility that Lisa would have access to Murray's old car if they'd been together when he got tossed into the slammer, and that would point to her being the one who came to Paula's house and the one who tried to get in here the night of our barbecue."

Trent slid back his chair and stood.

Henry was immediately on his feet too, striding hopefully toward the door.

"Let me help you clean up," Trent said, "and then let's take this poor animal for a walk. Maybe we could put him on a leash."

I snorted. "Never had a cat, did you?"

Henry stood on his hind legs and batted at the door knob.

Trent set the box with the leftover pizza in the refrigerator and looked at Henry. "No cats, just dogs."

"Cats and leashes don't mix well. I'll tell you what you could do if you really want to help Henry. Take Lisa and Rick in for questioning. You can hold them for twenty-four hours without filing charges. I saw that on TV. With them safely in custody, I can let Henry roam and check out his territory."

I tried to pick him up and console him—Henry, not Trent—but he was having none of that and squirmed out of my arms.

Trent sighed. "I can't bring them in without some kind of evidence. You'll just have to give Henry some more catnip."

"Is that your solution for everything? Drugs? Really?"

He reached for the plates we'd used, but I jerked them away and took them to the sink myself. "I ask you for one little favor, put my ex-husband and his girlfriend in jail for one stinking night, and you won't do it. You are so freaking uptight."

I glared at him.

He grinned at me. "And you are so freaking loosey-goosey. Let's go sit down and talk." He tried to take my hand, but I pulled it away.

"We've been sitting and talking. At least, *I've* been talking, telling you everything I know, practically solving your case for you, and all you do is tell me to give Henry more catnip."

"Look, I think you may have some valid points, but I'm going to have to do a little investigating

181

before I haul anybody off to jail. Unlike you and Fred, I have to follow the rules."

I rolled my eyes. "Yes, I know. It's always about the rules. Don't you ever want to just go wild and break the rules?"

He grinned and gave me a sizzling head-to-toe look, the green in his brown eyes flaring. "Yeah, sometimes I do want to go wild and break the rules."

"Really?" I squeaked.

"Let's go sit in the living room and break some rules."

"Really?" It was all I could think of to say. I'd been waiting for this moment for a long time. However, even though Trent wasn't the romantic type, I'd expected it to be a little more romantic than an invitation to sit in the living room and break rules.

"Yeah," he said. "Get some chocolate, and while we have dessert I'll tell you something official about this case that I really shouldn't tell you."

"Oh." I was glad he was going to tell me something official. I was glad this wasn't going to be the not-very-romantic culmination I'd first thought. Well, I was half-way glad.

# Chapter Eighteen

I let Trent take my hand and lead me to the living room. Henry followed our every step. He was no longer a free, independent creature. He was in prison as surely as George Murray was in prison.

Trent and I sat on the sofa while Henry strode to the front door and stretched up, making his increasingly familiar attempt to open the door. He meowed a couple of times to be sure we saw him. Like anybody would fail to notice a large white cat stretched over three feet from his rump to his front paws, desperately trying to get a grip on my cut glass door knob with those huge paws.

"I'm sorry, sweetie," I said. "Soon, I promise."

"You never call me *sweetie*," Trent observed.

I leaned close to him. "Henry doesn't keep secrets from me. Tell me all your secrets, and maybe I'll call you *sweetie*."

He arched an eyebrow in disbelief. "We'll soon see. I should not be telling you this, so I'd appreciate it if you wouldn't repeat any of it to Fred."

I said nothing, my mind completely occupied with figuring out how I'd get around that admonition and pass the information along to Fred without actually breaking Trent's trust.

He sighed. "Oh, never mind. Just don't tell anybody else except Fred, okay?"

Damn. That meant Fred would have to tell Paula. "Okay," I agreed.

"I'm only telling you this because it links to what you've already deduced."

"Yeah, yeah, yeah. I absolve you of all guilt, blah, blah, blah. So tell me!"

"Diane Hartman says she's innocent of Bradford's murder. Of course, they all say that. But Diane claims she and Bradford never really broke up, that his marriage to Lisa was part of a scam to get hold of a large amount of money. She doesn't know the details. He just told her there was nothing between Lisa and him, that he only married her because she insisted on it as a part of the deal, and as soon as they got the money, he'd take all of it, dump her, and he and Diane would move to Mexico."

I leaned back on the sofa, pulling my knees up and wrapping my arms around them. "Wow. Everybody's betraying everybody."

"That happens when a lot of money and a lot of dishonest people are involved."

Henry leapt gracefully onto the sofa and lay down beside me. I stroked him from head to tail. He growled for a moment, but soon settled into purring. I'd have to remember that technique for possible use on Trent when he growled at me next time.

"Pretty much confirms that Lisa and Rick killed Bradford," I said, still having a little difficulty wrapping my mind around the picture of Rick the Murderer. "Besides the element of greed, they could have found out about Diane and what Bradford planned to do."

"That's what I'm thinking. Especially after what you told me, I believe Diane didn't kill Bradford, but I'm a little concerned about releasing her. What if your ex-husband and his new girlfriend decide she's a threat, that maybe she knows too much? They're on a roll. They've killed Bradford, they've broken into your house and now they tried to burn down your restaurant."

"So you believe me about the restaurant, that it was no accident?"

He wrapped both arms around me. I set my feet back on the floor so I could get closer. "Of course I believe you," he said. "And now I'm even more worried about you."

I pulled away and looked at him. "Are we going to start that sleeping on the couch business again? Cause I got to tell you, I'm not in favor of that idea. Death by Chocolate is closed for the next few days, I don't have to get up early, and I can spend the entire night stomping up and down the stairs, playing loud music and keeping you awake."

He held up his hands in a gesture of surrender. "Fine. So I'll leave you here alone, and if you wake up dead tomorrow, we'll never have the chance to make love."

He did have a point.

"I'll sleep with my iron skillet and two knives on my nightstand, and I'll put chairs under the knobs on the front and back doors and my bedroom door. If anybody tries to break in, I'll hear them and call you immediately."

"Call Fred first. He's closer."

"My first call will be to Fred." Right after I used the iron skillet to bludgeon Rick.

I finally persuaded Trent to leave. Who knew I'd ever be trying to get a hot guy to leave instead of spending the night? Just goes to show, you never know. But I couldn't wait to get Trent out of there so I could call Fred.

"This time," I said as soon as he answered, "I'm the one with new information."

"You badgered Trent until he finally told you about Diane and Bradford's scheme to cut Lisa out of the money?"

Damn! "Do you have my house bugged?"

"Why would I do that?"

Of course I wasn't going to get a simple *yes* or *no* out of him.

"I think we should go back to visit the Murrays, the ones that aren't in prison," I said. "See if they know anything about their grandson's love life."

"Precisely what I was thinking."

"Were not."

"Was too. I'll call them tomorrow." He hung up.

I did actually bar all the doors with chairs before I went to bed, and it felt really creepy to be doing that in order to keep my almost-ex-husband from breaking in to slit my throat.

\*\*\*

The senior Murrays were thrilled we were coming for another visit. I felt a little guilty since we were only going over to grill them about their grandson, but Fred assured me they knew that and were happy we were coming anyway. So I made a Triple Chocolate Cake, and we returned to Summerdale Retirement Village at a few minutes after three the following afternoon. That gave Harold time to finish his round of golf.

Cathy and Harold met us at the door. "Come in," she said, holding the door wide and offering an even wider smile. "We're delighted you all came back to see us again."

We entered, and I handed her the covered cake plate. "It's chocolate," I said.

She took it and laughed, the sound clear and pure like tiny bells. "Of course it is. Oh, my goodness, it weighs a ton! This must be really rich." Then she sobered. "I heard about your restaurant fire on the news. Have a seat, and I'll get some drinks. Coffee and Coke, right?"

"Right."

She set the cake on the coffee table and headed for the kitchen.

Harold took his seat in the same chair as before, and Fred and I sat on the sofa. "Cathy loves to entertain," Harold said, "especially young people. Some of these folks around here are a lot older than they ought to be, if you know what I mean."

"Harold," Cathy called from the kitchen, "can you come help me?"

Harold rose. "Excuse me. Can't say no to my lady." He winked and left the room.

I looked at Fred. "Must be a really big cup of coffee."

Harold returned, staggering slightly under the weight of a large tray holding a silver coffee pot, three cups, a platter of snacks, four small plates, silverware, and a can of Coke. He set the tray on the coffee table and resumed his seat.

"We didn't expect all this," I protested.

"Of course you didn't," Cathy said. "It wouldn't be a surprise if you'd expected it. I thought we'd have a little afternoon tea without the tea. Your cake will be a perfect addition." She lifted the top to expose the tall, dark cake dusted with powdered sugar. "Oh, my, that looks good!" She took a knife from the tray and sliced four generous pieces.

I looked at Fred helplessly.

He smiled at Mrs. Murray. "What a wonderful surprise. It looks delicious." He took a plate and helped himself to some of everything.

I followed suit, and Cathy poured three cups of coffee.

Fred bit into a stuffed mushroom. "This is delicious. Do I detect a hint of tarragon?"

Cathy beamed. "Why, yes, you do! That's my own special recipe, but I'll be happy to share."

"Thank you. I'll take you up on that offer."

My cell phone began to play George Strait's *Blue Clear Sky*, Trent's ring tone. I flinched. "Sorry. I didn't think about turning it off. Nobody ever calls this time of day. I'm usually at work."

"Go right ahead and take your call," Cathy said. "We don't stand on formalities here."

"I can return the call later."

We ate and drank and talked and laughed, and I forgot our reason for being there until Fred brought it up.

He set his empty plate on the tray, refreshed his cup of coffee and sat back. "We visited your grandson yesterday."

Cathy smiled wistfully. "That was nice of you. He doesn't get many visitors, mostly just Harold and me."

"I'm not sure he enjoyed our visit," I said. "When I mentioned that Lisa Whelan might be moving into your old house, he got a little upset. Was she his girlfriend?"

Cathy set her cup on the coffee table and looked at her husband. "Was that her name, that exotic dancer he had in the car that night?"

Harold's brow furrowed in thought. "I think so." He turned his gaze to Fred and me. "He never talked much about the women he dated, never brought them over to meet us. He was pretty secretive about that part of his life."

"He was secretive about most parts of his life," Cathy said.

Harold nodded. "The only time we ever saw him with a woman was one evening when he stopped by to borrow some money. There was a blond woman with him. He came to the door but she just stood out by the car."

"We asked him to bring her inside," Cathy said. "It was about this time of year and hot. We said we'd love to meet her. We wouldn't have criticized. We'd have accepted anyone he cared about, but he refused. I'm pretty sure he called her Lisa."

"Was she blonde?" Fred asked.

"Yes," Cathy said. "I don't believe it was her natural hair color, though. She looked like those movie stars that were so popular when I was young."

"Marilyn Monroe?"

"Yes. Marilyn Monroe, Jayne Mansfield, those women."

"Pretty girl," Harold added.

Cathy nodded. "She was pretty."

"Did she have…" I hesitated, not sure how to phrase my inquiry and not sound crude.

"Was she amply endowed?" Fred asked.

"Yes." Harold blushed and slid his gaze to his wife.

Cathy laughed and patted his hand. "You can look all you want as long as you don't touch."

He grinned sheepishly.

"George never mentioned any other women?" Fred asked.

Harold and Cathy both shook their heads.

"How about since he's been in prison? Has he mentioned a woman whose first name begins with K?" Fred asked.

Cathy shook her head again. "We do most of the talking when we visit him. He seems very unhappy, but who wouldn't be unhappy in a terrible place like that?"

"I've been talking to him about learning a legitimate trade when he gets out," Harold said. "Told him we'd help him if he wanted to go back to school. He's young enough, he could start a new life." He sighed. "He doesn't seem very interested in that idea."

Cathy patted his hand. "But you never know when something you say is going to make a difference. He may seem disinterested, but he hears everything you tell him, and one day it will all come back to him and influence the way he lives the rest of his life. Most important thing, he knows we love him and we're here for him."

We chatted and drank for a while longer. Trent called again and I ignored him again. It wasn't like him to call two times in a row like that. Usually he'd leave a message and wait for me to call him back. But it would be rude to take a phone call during a visit.

Fred got Cathy's recipe for stuffed mushrooms, and finally we headed out the door.

"I hope you'll come back to visit again." Cathy gave both of us a hug. "We'd love to have you over for dinner."

"I grill a mean steak," Harold said.

"That would be great. We'd love to come, but only if you'll come to my house—your old house—for dinner." The words that came out of my mouth surprised me since I didn't know I was going to say them until I did, but I realized I meant them. I liked the Murrays and would enjoy seeing them again. "I make a mean chocolate chip cookie."

Cathy smiled. "I have a feeling anything you make will taste wonderful."

Fred shook Harold's hand. "Her coffee's terrible."

"But Fred makes great coffee. Between the two of us, we'll put it together."

Cathy put an arm around her husband's waist. "We'd love to see our home again."

"Then it's a done deal," I said. "How about this Saturday? With my restaurant closed, I'll have plenty of time to cook. I might even clean."

Harold laughed. "Don't go to too much trouble. We want to recognize the old place."

"Harold!" Cathy gave him a mock glare.

I entertained a fleeting thought that perhaps Trent and I would be like them one day.

Nah. My glare would be real.

"Seven on Saturday," I confirmed. "And the guy I'm sort of seeing will probably be there too."

"Looking forward to it," Cathy said.

As we drove away, my phone rang again. Trent, for the third time. I decided to answer.

"Hello?"

"Lisa's been murdered. Her trailer was burned to the ground with her in it, and Rick was seen leaving there shortly before the fire. I've brought him in for questioning."

# Chapter Nineteen

As soon as we got home, I opened the door and let Henry run. He darted out onto the front porch but then turned back and looked at me as if not quite sure he was really going to be allowed to do this.

"Go on," I said. "Lisa's dead, and Rick's in jail. Enjoy! Just be sure you come back before morning. And don't get in any fights!" He was already off the porch and vanished into the early evening shadows before he heard that last. Not that it made any difference. He'd been away for a while and would likely have to defend his territory against interlopers.

"Anlinny!" I looked up to see Zach racing across the yard toward me. I squatted and scooped him up in a big hug. "My truck broke but Mommy got me a new one and it's red and I played with it while Mommy cooked macaroni and cheese and we ate it." At least, I think that's what he said. His speech was still a little garbled. He could have said he'd played with a brick and they'd eaten marbles and geese.

Mommy was close behind, of course. "Fred just called about Rick. I'm so sorry."

I set Zach down so he could do his Taz imitation around the yard. "You're sorry?" I asked. "Because they caught him?"

"No, and you know that's not what I'm saying. You cared about him once. Even if you don't anymore, it's hard to accept that somebody you loved and trusted can do something so horrible."

I nodded. Paula knew all about that. Her ex had tried to steal Zach and kill me. "I think I'm past the shock," I said.

"Are you? Why don't we go inside and have a glass of wine, maybe two."

"Sure." I spotted Zach running in circles around a tree. "Zach, want some wine?"

"Yes!" He ran toward the house, dashed between Paula and me and went inside the house. That boy loves his wine.

Paula turned to follow him. "I hope my future daughter-in-law isn't a wine connoisseur. I can just see their wedding when Zach proposes a toast with a glass of grape juice."

I opened a fresh box of white zin for Paula and me and poured some juice into the red sippy cup I kept at my place for Zach. He could do a lot worse than toasting his bride—a woman who wouldn't be good enough for him anyway—with a glass of grape juice.

I brought out a yellow truck for Zach, and he starting zooming it around the floor. Paula and I settled on the sofa. I closed only the screen door, letting the warm—okay, hot—breeze drift in with the soft sounds of evening…the laughter of kids playing, the bark of a dog, the noise of a cat fight. I relaxed at the familiar noises. Losing my home was no longer a threat, and my cat was enjoying himself. Life was good.

I took a long sip of my wine before speaking. "I'm okay with Rick going to prison for murder," I said. "Really."

"Really?"

"Okay, it's kind of weird. I've never known anybody who committed murder and arson and—" I flung my arms wide. "Who knows what else?"

She shrugged. "I once thought I'd committed murder."

"Even if you had killed David, that would have been like stepping on a rabid brown recluse spider just as it tried to bite you."

Paula frowned. "I don't think spiders get rabies."

"Now you're starting to sound like Fred. You know what I mean."

She grinned and sipped her drink. "Yeah, I do. And you know what I mean. This whole thing with Rick and Lisa and that man dying outside our restaurant has got to be bothering you."

I let out a long sigh and drained my non-crystal wine glass. Having close friends is great except when they insist on being close. I examined the feelings I didn't want to examine. "The Rick that tried to burn down Death by Chocolate and killed that woman is not the same Rick I married. Well, he probably is, but I didn't know it. I married Rick because he was fun and because my parents didn't like him. It broke my heart when I caught him with Muffy and he said he loved her and wanted a divorce. But even before that, I'd noticed signs that he was not the person I thought

I married. I just kept hoping he'd become that fictional person again."

I stood. My glass was empty while Paula's was still full. I'd have to fix that inequity. I went to the kitchen to refill my glass.

Zach charged in and held up his sippy cup. "More wine!" I poured juice for him, cheap wine for me, and we both returned to the living room.

Paula looked up as I came in. "Now you've learned he has a dark side even you never suspected."

"Determined I'm going to face this, are you?" I plopped onto the sofa and drew in a deep breath. "Yes, I'm freaked out that he could be capable of such terrible crimes, although some of his real estate deals were a little shady. I guess it's only a short step to go from scamming a few extra fees to taking a person's life." A horrible thought occurred to me. "He's going to need an attorney. I hope he doesn't ask Dad or one of the partners at Dad's firm to defend him."

"Surely not. Your dad only does real estate law. He won't even get you out of your speeding tickets."

"Yeah, but he and Rick have become sort of friendly enemies since we split up. My parents will be back from their cruise on Monday. Who knows what they'll do when they find out everything that's been going on? They've kind of bonded with Rick in their common belief that the divorce is all my fault because I'm irresponsible and undependable."

Paula didn't reply.

"Hey!" I sat upright and looked at her. "As my best friend, this is the point where you jump in and assure me that's not true."

"Of course it's not true." She said that way too easily. "I was just wondering why he did it."

"Why?" I hadn't actually considered that question.

"Yes, why? If the two of them had a plan to get your house and find a lot of money, and she was the one with the information, why would he kill her?"

"Who knows? Maybe she was going to dump him the way she dumped Murray."

"She couldn't. She had no money. She was dependent on him to get your house. I don't know. It's not adding up."

"We need to get Mr. Computer Head involved in this discussion. He'll sort out the pieces." I set my wine on the table, went to the front door and opened the screen to go outside and over to Fred's.

Rick stood on my porch. Even in the dusk of evening, I could see he looked pale and rumpled.

"What are you doing here?" I looked past him to see if my yard might be full of cops come to capture him and take him back to jail. "They arrested you for murder. You should be behind bars."

"No, they didn't arrest me. That boyfriend of yours took me in for questioning. They couldn't hold me. I haven't done anything wrong." He shoved his hands into his pockets and shifted from one foot to the other. "I need to talk to you. Can I come inside?"

"No. I have company."

He shrugged. "It's almost Zach's bedtime so they'll be leaving soon."

"How did you know Paula and Zach were here? Have you been eavesdropping?"

He got a *busted* expression on his face. Didn't happen often that The Conman was busted. I savored the moment. "I heard their voices, that's all," he said.

"You were eavesdropping! My mother would have you beaten and shunned if she knew that. Get off my porch. Go away. No, you can't come inside." I turned back into the room and found Paula standing directly behind me.

"Talk to her, Paula," Rick begged. "You said it yourself, I had no reason to kill Lisa. She and I had a business deal."

"What do you want, Rick?" Paula's voice was firm and cold.

"I need to talk to my wife."

"Oh, here we go with the *wife* business again! Get off my porch!" I shouted.

Rick took a step backward and held up his hands. "Okay, okay. I realize I don't have the right to call you that any longer, but please let me have just a few minutes of your time so I can explain and apologize."

"Apologize? I think I'm going to puke."

"Puke?" Zach repeated, coming up to the screen door and pressing his face against the mesh. Great. I'd taught him another new word to add to his Lindsay vocabulary of words like damn, freaking, bloody, and a few other colorful phrases his mother didn't really care for.

I turned back to Paula. "Go ahead and take Zach home. I'll talk to Psycho Man."

Paula pulled Zach close to her as if to protect him. "I don't think that's a good idea."

"Neither do I, but I'll do whatever it takes to get this jerk off my porch." And I wanted to hear more about his business deal with Lisa.

Paula reluctantly agreed. If she'd been alone and not responsible for Zach's safety, she'd probably have insisted on staying. "I'll call you every ten minutes, and if you don't answer, I'll call 911."

"I got a better idea." I walked over to my purse lying on the floor, retrieved my cell phone and punched in a number. "Fred? Rick's at my house. If I don't call you in thirty minutes, would you please come over here with your machine gun and blow him away?"

"What makes you think I have a machine gun?" I heard Fred's response, but Rick didn't.

"Thank you," I said, disconnected the call and smiled at Rick. "You have thirty minutes."

Paula and Zach left, and Rick came in. Again I closed only the screen, leaving the wooden door open. "So Fred won't have to blow it away. I hate it when he does that."

Rick sat on the sofa and looked at my glass. "Got any more wine?"

"Yes."

"I could sure use some."

I started to refuse, but then decided I might get more information out of him if he was drunk. I went

199

to the kitchen and filled a plastic glass with wine then gave it to him.

"Thank you, Lindsay." He drank half the glass in one gulp and made a face. He'd never cared for my taste in wine.

I took a seat in my recliner and made no move to reclaim my glass. I needed all my wits about me to deal with a murderer.

"I didn't kill Lisa," he said. "Can you close that door and turn on the air? It's hot in here." He was sweating.

"I'm comfortable. The door stays open." I looked at my watch. "Twenty-six minutes. You know how precise Fred is about everything."

"Look, I'm sorry we tried to take your house. Okay? Lisa said her old boyfriend hid a lot of money somewhere in this house. But, in my defense, I was offering you twice what the house was worth."

Finally I knew what everybody was looking for. Money supposedly hidden in my house. "*You* were offering? So the purchase price would have come from your assets?"

Rick shifted uncomfortably and drank some more of the wine he didn't like. "Lisa and Bradford came to me with a business deal. I'd front them the purchase price, and they'd share the money we found with me."

"So you were offering to pay me twice what this house is worth using money that's community property and half mine anyway?"

He almost looked embarrassed at being caught. Almost, but not quite. Rick the Salesman always has a comeback. "We'd have returned the place to you after we found the money."

"There's no money. Fred's gone over this house, basement to attic. Nothing. You're too late. Lisa came in and dug it up the day Bradford was killed." Even though Fred and I had concluded it couldn't have been Lisa who'd found the money, I couldn't resist the opportunity to gouge Rick. "You've been scammed, Mr. Kramer, just like you've done to so many people. Karma can be a bitch."

Rick shook his head. "Lisa didn't break in here, and she didn't find the money. She didn't know where it was. Bradford got Murray to admit that he'd hidden the money in his grandparents' house, but then Murray found out that Bradford and Lisa were working together, and he clammed up. Wouldn't tell Bradford where. That's why we needed to get the house. We were going to tear it down if we had to."

"And then give it back to me?"

"What?"

"You said you were going to return this place to me after you found the money. What you meant was, you'd give me back a pile of rubble, right?"

He swallowed and moved his fingers to his throat to loosen an imaginary tie. He was wearing a Polo shirt, so that didn't work very well.

"Were you here the whole time Fred was searching your house?" he asked.

"No. He did it while I was at work."

Rick beamed and shot up from the sofa. "That's it! Fred found the money and kept it for himself."

"Sit down, you moron. That's ridiculous. I trust Fred completely, and besides, he's already rich." He might be.

Rick sank down again. "Lisa didn't break into your house and she didn't get the money." He drew in a deep breath. "But she did set fire to Death by Chocolate."

I clenched my fists. "Now that poor little Lisa's dead, you're going to put all the blame on her?"

"It was all her! I had nothing to do with the fire. Why would I burn down a restaurant I own half of?"

"So I'd give you this house." But I was no longer so certain of his guilt.

He clasped his hands in his lap, looked down at them and shook his head. "It was all her doing. She came up with the idea, said if you lost your source of income, you'd have to sell the house to us. But I told her, absolutely not. I told her we were not going to harm you or cause you any problems."

"You are such a decent human being."

He smiled as if he thought I really meant it. "When you called and told me what had happened, I knew she'd done it anyway. I went to her place and confronted her. She admitted it, said she took the key off my key ring one night when she was at my place and I was asleep. She didn't know what time you went to work, so she didn't realize you'd catch the fire before it got out of control. That proves I had nothing to do with it. I know how early you go to work."

I slammed a fist onto the chair arm. "You told her not to do it, so you think that absolves you of guilt? You got involved with that woman, so you're just as responsible as she is." I reached over and retrieved my glass of wine from the coffee table. I needed something to calm me. Trent was right. If I'd had a gun at that moment, I might have shot Rick.

He straightened and looked me in the eye. "When Lisa admitted what she'd done, we had a big fight and I left. Somebody saw me leaving, and that's why the cops are trying to pin her murder on me. But I didn't do it. She was alive when I left. So that leaves the question of who burned down Lisa's trailer and killed her."

I opened my mouth, closed it, opened it again and drained my wine. "I don't like the way you're looking at me. Are you suggesting I had something to do with it?"

"I told you I was divorcing you so I could marry Lisa."

"And you think I'd kill her out of jealousy?" I burst into laughter.

Rick wilted. "Probably not."

"Maybe her fire was an accident, like the cops said mine was."

He shook his head. "They found gasoline everywhere. It was deliberate."

"I was being sarcastic."

"Meowr."

I looked at the door and saw a ghostly white figure with blue eyes standing on the other side. "Henry! You're home!" I got up and let him in. I expected him to go straight to the kitchen for food and water after his evening on the town, but instead he leaped onto the sofa and sat down a cushion away from Rick, watching him intently. My knight in white fur.

"Don't make any sudden moves," I warned Rick. "He hasn't eaten yet."

Rick licked his lips nervously. "There's money somewhere in your house," he said, never taking his gaze off Henry. "About ten million dollars, give or take a few thousand. We just need to find it, and we'll both be rich."

I gulped. "Ten *million*? Are you sure? That's an awful lot of money."

"I'm sure. Lisa was with Murray when he stole it from the drug dealers."

I sat bolt upright. "It's drug money? This story just gets worse with every word that comes out of your mouth. Bad enough you got involved with an arsonist, but those drug people are dangerous!"

"Relax. Nobody knows Murray took it."

"Excuse me? He's in prison! Somebody knows!"

"No, no. He and Lisa ran a scam on two big time drug dealers, and each one thought the other one took the money. Murray's in prison because she turned him in. After it all came down, after she put her life on the line and helped him, he refused to give her half. He was going to keep it all and run away with his new girlfriend."

"His new girlfriend? Murray had a new girlfriend before he went to prison? He dumped Lisa, not the other way around?"

"Yeah, he dumped her for another stripper. People like him just don't have any morals."

I was too interested in what he was saying to upbraid him for his hypocrisy about morals. "There's another woman involved in this? Is she tall and blonde?"

"How would I know?"

I shook my head and sat back in my chair. "I don't suppose you would know or care. So Murray dumped Lisa, refused to give her the money she helped him steal, and she turned him in to the cops?"

"Yeah, she called in an anonymous tip and reported him for having drugs in his car. He did, of course. She got even with him, but it didn't help her find the cash. Then she got in contact with Murray's cellmate, Rodney Bradford, and made a deal with him. If he'd find out from Murray where the money was, when he got out, they'd get married and split it."

"I see. He got out and told her it was in this house. But neither of them had the money to buy the place, so they tracked the house to you and enlisted your aid."

He shrugged and tried to look boyish and innocent. It was a good attempt, but I knew him too well. "Then Bradford died, and Lisa and I tried to carry on."

"You *tried to carry on*? That's an interesting way to put it."

"Hey, it's not like that. Lisa and Bradford weren't in love or anything. She only married him so she could throw it in Murray's face because he dumped her. She wanted to have the money and share it with another man the way he'd tried to share it with another woman."

"But it was the real thing with you and Lisa. You loved her. You were going to marry her."

"Oh, that. I told you, it was just a business deal. Lisa thought you'd feel better about letting me have the house if you believed it was romance. You have such a soft heart. That's one of the things I've always loved about you." He smiled. The jerk actually had the balls to smile.

"I understand. You were just looking for the easiest way to scam me out of my home."

"No!" He looked aghast. Well, he made an effort to look aghast. "It was a stupid scheme. I don't know what came over me. I've just been so upset with this crazy divorce you insist on going through with."

"Oh, do not twist this to try to make it sound like it's my fault you're a conniving jerk!"

He lowered his head in a mock gesture of contrition. "I'm sorry, Lindsay. I'm so sorry. Is there anything I can do to make this right?" He rose and took a step toward me. Henry made one of his jungle sounds, and Rick froze.

"Yes, there is," I said. "Sign the divorce papers."

Eying Henry nervously, Rick sat back down on the sofa. "Does everything we once had mean nothing? I've always loved you, and I always will."

"You don't, and you won't. Give it a rest. There's no money in this house, and if I do find any, I'll take it straight to the cops. You won't get even one coke-dusted hundred dollar bill."

He shot to his feet again, oblivious to Henry's snarls. "It's here! Murray told Bradford he hid the money here! If you don't have it and Fred didn't take it, ten million dollars is still hidden in this house, and my name is still on the title to this house!"

Fred kicked the door open and strode in with a machine gun.

# Chapter Twenty

Rick suddenly remembered an appointment and had to leave.

Fred leaned the machine gun against the wall and shook his head. "I never know what you're going to ask me to do next."

I rushed to the kitchen to get a Coke. Time for something stronger than wine.

I returned with two sodas, one for me and one for Fred. "Where did you get that?" I asked, indicating the intimidating hunk of metal.

"From my attic." He accepted the Coke and sat down on the sofa a cushion away from Henry. My guard cat relaxed and closed his eyes. The two might not be best buds, but they respected each other.

Fred hadn't really answered my question about the origin of the gun, but I knew there was no point in pursuing it. "Is it loaded?"

"I'll do a lot of things for you, Lindsay, but I refuse to blow away your ex-husband. I have no moral objection to the act, but it is illegal and a lot more trouble to get out of than a speeding ticket."

I was pretty sure that meant the gun wasn't loaded. I set my drink on the coffee table and moved over to examine it more closely. "Can I shoot it?"

"No."

I reached to pick it up. After all, I was pretty sure it wasn't loaded.

"I wouldn't do that. You'll get your fingerprints on it and then, if I do have occasion to shoot Rick, you'll be blamed."

I jerked my hand away from the gun. "You have a way of putting things in perspective." I returned to my chair and sat down. "I have news. I know some things you don't know."

"I'll know soon because you can't keep secrets."

He was absolutely right, so I didn't bother to waste time protesting. I told him everything Rick had revealed about Lisa's involvement in the theft and her scheme to get her hands on the money. "I feel kind of sorry for her," I admitted. "She lost her boyfriend and her share of the loot, she got involved with Rick, and now she's dead."

Fred sat quietly sipping his Coke. I could almost hear the hard drive in his brain spinning and whirring.

"It's got to be the new girlfriend," I said. "Murray told her where the money is."

Fred nodded but still said nothing.

"She broke in here and found the money."

Fred shook his head and finally spoke. "If she found the money, why did she come back again and why did she go to Paula's and ask about your financial state?"

"You think there's another person involved, somebody who got into my basement and dug up the money?"

"That's the logical conclusion."

I thought about the ramifications. "So that person wouldn't be trying to get back into my house, but the new girlfriend, the one who lost the earring, may not know somebody else has the money, so she's been returning, trying to find it."

I looked at Henry snoozing happily on the sofa after his run around the neighborhood. Damn! I didn't want to have to worry about him again, drug him and keep him inside all the time. In fact, I wasn't crazy about locking myself inside the house again and worrying about an intruder.

For a few minutes, neither of us said anything. Henry didn't snore. Even the sounds of the night were hushed. We were all thinking. I needed to put the pieces together, figure out who got the money and somehow let the new girlfriend know so she'd leave us alone.

"This other player, the one who found the money, it would have to be someone involved with Murray," I said, "someone he trusted enough to confide about the money. Another inmate? Maybe somebody who's killed before, somebody who'd be willing to murder Bradford and Lisa to keep them from getting to the cash first."

Fred drained his soda and set the can on the coffee table. His gaze behind his wire-rimmed glasses was distant as if his thoughts were far away. "Poison is an impersonal way to kill," he finally said. "However, Lisa's murder was personal."

"It was? What do you mean? How do you know that?" He was either being psychic or he'd hacked into the police files.

His gaze returned from outer space or wherever his thoughts had been. "The fire didn't kill her. Someone bashed in her head then stabbed her seventeen times. That's personal, an act of rage."

Yep, hacked into the police files. Again.

"You think it was the new girlfriend? Seems to me it would be more likely Lisa would want to hack up her replacement than the other way around."

"It's possible Lisa's trailer was searched before her murderer set fire to it, though it's impossible to be certain considering how messy her place already was and how much destruction the fire caused. Somebody could have thought she had the stolen money, then when she couldn't tell that person where it was, that person killed her and searched her trailer."

"Is there any way Lisa could have had the money and this woman found it during her search?" I wanted that to be true since it would mean an end to the danger for Henry, my house and me.

Fred looked at me. He didn't have to say anything. We both knew I was reaching.

"Not likely, is it? Couldn't have been Lisa or she wouldn't have been scrambling so desperately to get my house." I shuddered though the night air was quite warm. Hot, actually. "That means Murray's new girlfriend is a murderer who's looking for the money and killing anybody who gets in her way. She doesn't know about the first intruder, the guy who actually got the money. Now she probably thinks that Henry and I have the money and we're in her way."

He nodded slowly, his brow furrowed in thought.

"So we just need to find a tall, blonde stripper with big boobs and cat scratches, and all my problems will be over."

He nodded again.

I leaned forward, spreading my hands in disbelief. "I was being sarcastic! How do you propose we do that? Do you have any idea how many strip joints there are in this town? By the time we visit all of them, you're going to be too old to enjoy them."

"It won't be that difficult. We should start with the club where Lisa worked. Talk to her co-workers. Women talk about their heartaches. It's possible she told someone about Murray's treachery and whom he was cheating with."

"Possible," I admitted.

"I need to check the prison logs and see who's been to visit Murray besides his grandparents and us."

*Check the prison logs*? I wasn't even going to ask. "Good idea. Go do that right now, and we won't have to go to a strip club to find out this other woman's name."

He nodded. "I hope to find her name on the list, but it may be that she's now an ex-girlfriend. Let's assume Murray found out about Lisa and Bradford, so he knew they'd be going after his money. This second girlfriend, KD, also knew. He didn't want her to get it, so he confided in someone else, and that person got to the money first. That's another name I'd like to find."

"Yeah, well, that person has the money and he or she is perfectly happy and not causing any problems. I want to find the crazy woman who keeps trying to break into my house."

Fred rose from the sofa. "I'll go home and start searching. Tomorrow night you and I will visit Babes and More."

"Paula should go with us since she's the only one who's actually seen this woman."

Fred stopped at the door and turned back. "Zach can't go. You have to be twenty-one."

I rolled my eyes. "Of course Zach can't go. Why would you even think that?"

"Paula won't leave him alone."

"Oh. That's true. So I guess Paula and I will go, and you'll stay at home and babysit Zach."

That was fun. I got to see Fred look panic-stricken. He can easily take down a grown man wielding a gun, but kids and cats terrify him.

"You and I will go," he said firmly, "and if we get a lead on someone who may be the new girlfriend, we'll let Paula identify her later."

"Okay," I said. I often use that word as an abbreviation for the longer sentence, *It's okay if that's what you want to think, and I'm not going to argue with you, but I'm going to do as I please.*

As soon as Fred left, taking his machine gun with him, I went over to Paula's.

She opened the door wearing a robe. "Get dressed," I said. "We're going to a strip club."

"You've been drinking," she accused.

213

"A little. So you can drive." We went inside, and I explained the situation to her, told her what I'd learned from Rick and Fred. "We need to do this tonight. If that woman killed Lisa, she's liable to try the same thing with me, and Henry could get hurt defending me."

Paula bit her lip. I could see she was struggling. She tries to be a good friend and go along with whatever I ask of her even though she's basically a sane person. "I can't leave Zach."

"Fred will take care of him."

"Really? Fred agreed to babysit Zach?"

I headed toward the stairs. "I'll take him over while you change." Probably better she didn't see Fred's reaction.

I went up to Zach's room. He was lying in bed wide awake playing with his toes and talking to me on his toy phone. "Hi, Hot Shot. Uncle Fred wants you to spend a couple of hours with him, okay?"

Zach giggled and called Fred on his toy phone. Fred's communication channels are always a mystery. I was a little concerned Zach might actually connect to him.

Apparently that didn't happen because Fred was totally shocked when I arrived at his door with Zach in my arms. "I thought we agreed you and I would perform that activity tomorrow."

"You and I tomorrow, Paula and I tonight." I handed Zach to him and left. No point wasting time having a pointless argument.

"This discussion is not over!" he shouted at my back.

\*\*\*

I had anticipated that two women entering a strip club would be considered strange but no one gave us a second glance. Paula looked fairly normal. She had changed into slacks and a white shirt, but I still wore my cut-offs and a tee-shirt that said "Life is short, eat chocolate first." Nevertheless, no one seemed interested in us.

Loud music pounded through the dimly-lit room, and clouds of cigarette smoke created a haze that further obscured the tables and people. There were a couple of other female customers, both seated with men. A tall blonde woman slithered around a pole on a stage illuminated by a bright spotlight. The club wasn't crowded, and most of the men were seated as close to that stage as possible.

Paula and I took a seat at a chipped plastic table a few feet away.

"Is that her?" I asked, indicating the dancer as I leaned close to Paula's ear so she could hear me over the music.

Paula studied the woman then shrugged. "I don't know. I don't think so, but it's hard to tell. The woman who came to my house was wearing clothes."

A waitress appeared and put down two small paper napkins. "What can I get you to drink?"

"Coke," I said.

"Beer," Paula said. "In a bottle."

The waitress left.

"You don't like beer," I said.

"It comes in a bottle. I'm not sure they clean their glasses as thoroughly as we do."

My Coke came in a glass. I sat there pondering Paula's concern and not taking a sip.

"We need to talk to that dancer," Paula said. "If I can hear her voice, I'll know if she was the same one who pretended to be an insurance agent."

"That's not going to be easy with all this noise."

We took our drinks and moved up to the bar.

The dancer strutted closer to the customers, and men reached up to stuff money into her bra and G-string. She leaned over toward a couple of them, said something and laughed.

Fred had been right. I did need him. He'd know what to do.

But we'd left him home babysitting, so I'd have to figure it out. I reached into my purse and pulled out a five dollar bill.

Paula grabbed my arm. "What are you doing?"

"Giving her money so she'll talk to us. That seems to be the way it works."

"You can't do that! You can't put it in her—" She fluttered a hand. "Don't do that."

"I don't intend to." I waved the money in the air. "I'll just hand it to her. Chill. Have another beer."

"I don't like beer." She held up the still-full bottle.

The dancer, smiling voluptuously, came to our side of the stage and leaned over so I could stuff the money. I drew back. "No, no. Here. Take it. With your fingers. We need to talk to you."

She took the bill, mouthed "Thank you," and glided on to the next person with money.

"That went well," Paula said.

"Hey, sarcasm is my area. Stop encroaching."

We went back to the table and sat down.

Paula took a sip of her beer, made a face and set it on the table. "We might as well go home. Neither one of us has a clue how to do this."

I took a drink of my Coke, dirty glass be damned. It was flat. I could deal with a dirty glass but not a flat Coke. "We're not going home until we've talked to every girl in this place. We just have to figure out what Fred would do."

"He'd make up some outrageous story and get us in the dressing room so we could talk to the dancers in a quieter, more private atmosphere." The voice of reason.

"And that's exactly what we're going to do." I stood. "Come on. Follow my lead." I walked through the restaurant and out the front door then stopped on the sidewalk and drew in a deep breath. "Wow. You don't realize how great hot, muggy air feels and how wonderful quiet sounds until you spend some time surrounded by stale cigarette smoke and loud music."

Paula moved up to stand beside me. "I agree. Those poor girls are going to get lung cancer and hearing damage from dancing in there." She checked her watch. "It's nearly eleven. Maybe we should postpone this until another night."

I shook my head. "I refuse to hide in my own home any longer. We're going to find that woman and set her straight."

Two men walked down the sidewalk toward us, gave us appreciative glances, then went into the club.

"Come on," I said. "We're going in the back door like the other dancers."

Paula followed, grumbling. "I'm not sure this is such a good idea."

"I'm not sure either, but we'll soon find out."

We walked around the building to the alley and located the back door. I yanked on the handle and, to my surprise, it opened. "See? This is going to be easy. We should have tried this first. We could have saved five dollars and the price of two bad drinks."

We walked into a dimly lit corridor. The music was audible but not as loud as out front. I could hear women talking and laughing from a couple of lighted rooms that opened off the corridor.

No problem. Who needed Fred?

"Let's try that room over there," I said, pointing to the nearest doorway.

A huge man appeared out of nowhere, blocking our way. "Where do you think you're going?" He stood at least seven feet tall—okay, maybe not quite seven feet, but close. His massive head was completely bald, his eyebrows stood out a couple of inches as he glowered down at us, and his arms that were folded across his two-foot wide chest were the size of tree trunks.

I admit, I was a little intimidated at first. But again I asked myself, *What would Fred do?*

I folded my arms in imitation of his stance and tried to return his fierce expression. Somehow I don't think it had the same effect when I had to look up to do it. "Going to work," I squeaked. I cleared my throat and tried again. "I'm going to work. I'm the new stripper, Fire Dancer." I shook my red curls in what I hoped—but doubted—was an alluring movement.

His expression didn't change. "Nobody told me nothing about no new stripper."

"They always tell you everything that's going on?"

He thought about that for a minute. "No."

"Obviously this is one of those times. I've got my first show in half an hour. I need to get changed." I edged to one side, moving to go around him.

"Who's she?" He looked at Paula who'd been standing behind me.

Good question. My friend? My accomplice?

"My costume manager."

"Oh." He looked at me again, and his eyes dropped to my tee-shirt. I didn't think he was reading the words. "Are you sure—?"

I snapped my fingers. "Hey! Eyes front and center! You want me to report you?"

His expression changed to fear. "No."

We went around the man-mountain and headed for the first lighted door.

Fred would be so proud of me. If he ever spoke to me again after the way I'd dumped Zach on him.

# Chapter Twenty-One

A brunette and a blonde, both clad in flashy, scanty clothing, sat in front of lighted mirrors, talking while one dabbed her cheeks with a brush and the other spread glue from a tube onto a strip of long, black, glittery eyelashes. They both turned when Paula and I entered the room.

"I'm investigating the death of your former co-worker, Lisa Bradford," I said, trying to sound official. Probably should have worn something other than cut-offs and that tee-shirt if I wanted to look official.

The women went back to their business of enhancing their cheeks and eyes but not to the talking business.

"She was murdered this morning." I lowered my voice a couple of octaves in my effort to overcome the tee-shirt and cut-offs.

"We heard." The blonde pursed her lips and added bright red color.

I looked at Paula to see if she recognized the woman's voice. She shrugged.

"How well did you know the deceased?"

"We worked with her," the blonde said.

The brunette settled the glittering eyelash onto her right eye and turned her stool to face us. She looked a little lopsided with one normal eye and one glittering eye. "We knew Lisa as well as you can know someone under these circumstances. We have private lives, but in this job, we all form a bond with each other. It's us against them."

"*Them* being the customers?" I asked.

The blonde looked at me in the mirror but didn't turn around. "The customers, the bosses, everybody but us dancers."

I looked at Paula to see if the woman had spoken enough words for her to recognize or reject identification. Paula shrugged again.

"What's the matter with your little friend?" the blonde asked. "Can't she talk?"

"She's a trainee," I said. "They don't talk for the first year. Did all of you get along with Lisa?"

"Well enough." The brunette stood. She was tall, and her four-inch heels put her over six feet. She offered her hand. "I'm Deidre Madsen, and this is Gwen Copeland."

"Candy Cane," the blonde corrected.

I shook Deidre's hand. She had a firm grip. "Nice to meet you, Deidre, and, uh, Candy. I'm Lindsay Powell, and this is Paula Roberts."

Paula stepped forward to shake hands with Deidre too. She still didn't speak. Apparently she liked her identity as a mute trainee. Probably figured silence would equate to fewer charges of misconduct if we got caught.

Candy nodded but continued to gaze into the mirror, fluffing her already-fluffy hair.

221

"I'm afraid I can't tell you much, Officer Powell," Deidre said, returning to her seat.

I didn't correct her on the *officer* title, but I didn't confirm it either. Strictly speaking, I wasn't breaking any laws.

"Lisa was a very private person," Deidre continued. "She got along well with everybody, but she didn't share her personal life. The first any of us knew of her marriage was when we heard about her death."

I sighed. We were accomplishing exactly nothing. "She had a boyfriend a few years ago, George Murray. Did she ever talk about him?"

Deidre shook her head. "Not since I've known her, but I've only been here a little over a year."

"She's going to school," Candy said.

"Who? Lisa? What kind of school?"

Candy looked disgusted at my lack of comprehension. "No, not Lisa. Her." She indicated Deidre. "Sparkles."

Deidre gave us a half smile and pointed to her lone eyelash. "Sparkles. *Deidre* just doesn't have the proper zing. Besides, my mother would have a seizure if she found out. She thinks I'm putting myself through law school by tutoring other students."

A mother. Law school. My perspective on these women shifted. Lisa would have had a mother too. I'd have to check into that. Maybe she'd been closer to her mother than to her co-workers.

"I knew George," Candy said. "Big talker, little doer. He was always going to take Lisa away from this life." She snorted and turned to actually face us rather than viewing us second-hand in the mirror. "Lisa was doing just fine till she got hooked up with that man. She was a good dancer, and she got good tips. Had her own little place, a nice little mobile home she inherited from her dad. But George filled her head full of big ideas. They were gonna be rich, buy a big house, get a dog, have a baby. She quit work on his say-so, then he dumped her and she come crawling back here."

"Did she say why he dumped her?"

Candy stood, magnificent in her red and white striped regalia. "Another woman, of course. There's always another woman."

My heart rate sped up. Now we were getting somewhere! "Was she another stripper? Somebody you knew?"

Candy regarded me for a long moment, her blue eyes sharp and filled with knowledge she was probably not going to share. Unlike me, this woman kept secrets. "That's my music. I gotta go." She started out the door but turned back at the last minute. "Ask her sister."

"Her sister?" I started after her. "What's her name? Where does she live? How do I get hold of her?"

Candy continued striding down the hallway as if she didn't hear me.

Someone else heard me, though.

Trent stepped out of the second door, blocking my progress. "Lindsay? What are you doing here?"

A thousand possible responses raced through my mind.

*I was looking for a place to buy a gift for a baby shower, and my GPS brought me here to Babes and More.*

*I'm in charge of my high school reunion, and that woman was our head cheerleader.*

*With Death by Chocolate closed, I had to find a new career.*

I settled for the truth. "Looking for Lisa's murderer."

"Officer Powell, are you okay?" Deidre stood in the hallway. "Is this man bothering you? I can call Ralph to get rid of him."

Even in the dim hallway I could see Trent's face flush a dark red. "I'm not bothering you, am I, *Officer* Powell?" He flipped out his badge and held it up for Deidre to see. "Adam Trent. *Detective* Adam Trent."

Deidre smiled. "You two know each other?"

Something in the way she smiled or maybe it was the twinkle in her dark eyes told me she knew I was no officer, that she'd known all along. I, the Queen of Sarcasm, had failed to recognize it coming from someone else. How humiliating.

"Could I have a few minutes of your time, Miss—?" Trent asked.

"Deidre Madsen. Certainly, Detective Trent. Can we talk while I finish putting on my costume? I'm up after Candy." She went back into her dressing room.

"Of course." He leaned inside the other doorway. "Lawson, I'll be next door when you're finished in here."

Great. Stone Face and Granite Man at the same time, and me without a single chocolate chip cookie to bribe them.

Trent followed me to Deidre's dressing room. He kept his hand on my waist the entire time as if he thought I might try to escape.

"Well, Officer Powell," he said when we were inside the room, "I see you brought Officer Roberts."

Paula, standing as close as she could get to the corner of the room and looking even smaller than she actually was, let out a strangled sound.

"I'm surprised Officer Sommers isn't here too."

"He's, um, with Officer Zachary."

Trent and I were probably going to have a discussion about this later, a loud discussion.

Deidre applied her other sparkly eyelash and watched us in the mirror. Her eyes were as sparkly as her lashes. She might not know exactly what was going on, but I suspected she had a pretty good idea. Sharp lady, and she was going to be a lawyer. I made a mental note of her name for future reference.

Trent took out his little notebook and his pen. "Can I get your legal name, residence address and phone number, ma'am?"

She gave him the information. I repeated the phone number to myself nine times. I've heard that's what it takes to commit something to memory.

"Were you acquainted with Lisa Whelan Bradford?"

"Yes, I knew her, but, as I told Officer Powell, I've only been here for a year."

"Want me to catch you up?" I asked Trent. "Or do you want to be redundant?"

"I'll be redundant, if that's okay with you."

I shrugged. "Then Officer Roberts and I might as well leave and begin our investigation based on the information we have."

Trent looped his arm through mine, holding me securely in place while he continued to write in that book of his. "I think you should both stick around. We can compare notes later."

He asked Deidre a few more questions but got no more information. Considering what a jerk he was being, I wasn't sure I was going to share the lead about Lisa's sister. After all, I'd offered to catch him up and he'd turned me down.

"What do you know about Lisa's sister?" Trent asked.

Damn. Somebody else had already blabbed.

"I didn't even know she had a sister until Candy mentioned her a few minutes ago. That's my music. I need to go." She rose, tossed back her dark, shiny hair and moved gracefully across the room then out the door, looking elegant in her ridiculous costume. Some people have the elegant gene and some of us have the chocolate gene.

"You are in so much trouble," Trent said.

I yanked my arm away from him. "No, I'm not. You are." The best defense is a good offense.

His eyes widened. "Me? What am I in trouble for? You're the one impersonating an officer!"

226

I shoved my fists onto my hips and glared at him. "I did no such thing. She assumed I was an officer, and I just didn't correct her. Ask the guard. I came in here pretending to be a stripper. I don't think you'll find any laws against a woman pretending to be a stripper."

Paula stepped up into the line of fire. "It's true, Trent. She never claimed to be an officer."

He shoved his notebook back inside his jacket and shook his head. "I'm sorry she got you involved in this, Paula."

My friend straightened and suddenly seemed several inches taller. "Don't be rude, Trent. If you didn't keep so many secrets from her, she wouldn't feel the need to do these things on her own."

That shut him up.

"What's the sister's name?" I asked. Never hurts to ask.

"I can't discuss the details—"

I interrupted him to complete that sentence. "—of an ongoing investigation, blah, blah, blah. Fine. I'll find out on my own."

His jaw clenched, and I knew he was grinding more enamel off his teeth.

"If you don't relax, you're going to have some big-time dental bills," I advised.

"I've got to finish up here right now, but you and I will talk tomorrow."

I tossed my hair, though it probably didn't come across as elegantly as Deidre's hair toss. "Assuming I'm speaking to you tomorrow. Let's go, Paula." I was glad to have the time to prepare some chocolate and some excuses.

We passed the big guy on our way out. I assumed he was Ralph.

"You leaving already?" he asked.

"I didn't get the job."

He glanced at my tee-shirt again. "Maybe you should get some of those implant things."

"Nah. I think I'll just find another career. Maybe I'll open my own restaurant."

"I've heard that's a tough thing to do."

"I've heard the same thing."

Paula and I drove home and discussed what we'd accomplished. Other than making Trent mad, we hadn't done a lot, and making Trent mad is no great accomplishment. I do it all the time without even trying.

"But we did learn that Lisa has a sister. Fred will be able to find out her name," I said confidently. "And he'll tell me, and then I'll tell Trent just so he'll know that I know."

"I'm not taking up for Trent," Paula said, "but you do sometimes push his buttons."

I smiled. "I do, don't I?"

We arrived at Fred's house shortly before midnight. He met us at the door before we had time to ring the bell or knock. His hair was mussed, his glasses were on crooked, and his eyes were wild. Zach must be suffering from insomnia. Actually, it was more likely Fred was suffering from Zach's insomnia.

The short person in question appeared behind him, beating a maroon Le Creuset pan with a wooden spoon. As soon as he saw Paula, he tossed both to the floor. "Mommy!" He ran to her, and she picked him up. "We saw women with no clothes and I played with Uncle Fred's 'puter and we had ice cream!"

Paula's eyes widened at his announcement, but she let it go. "Thank you for taking care of him, Fred." She crossed the yards to her house, holding Zach while he babbled excitedly.

Fred and I stood watching until she was safely inside.

"Had a good time, did he?" I asked, walking inside and taking a seat on his sofa. "I understand about the naked women, but I can't believe you let him play on your computer. You're so OCD about that."

Fred closed the door and straightened his glasses. "*Let him?* We were in the kitchen, and I was scooping out ice cream for him. When I turned to hand it to him, he was gone. I found him on my computer, checking out a porn website. I'll be getting emails for penile implants and cheap Viagra for the next ten years."

He sat down beside me, and I patted his hand. "There, there. It's going to be all right. Just hit the *delete* button when they come in."

"This is your fault. I hope you got enough information to justify my discomfort."

"Sort of. I found out Lisa has a sister, so now you just need to find out her name."

A smug expression settled on his face, looking very much at odds with his hair. "Her name is Kristen Delaney. She's Murray's only other visitor."

"Kristen Delaney? KD like the initials on Murray's tattoo? Murray dumped Lisa for her sister?"

# Chapter Twenty-Two

"Step sister," Fred clarified.

"Close enough. I can see the potential here for some big time animosity."

"If she's the one who killed Lisa by bashing out her brains and then stabbing her seventeen times, I'd definitely call that animosity."

"*If*? You don't think she did it?"

"Yes, I think she did it. As I said, that killing was personal. Stabbing someone that many times after they're already dead shows a lot of rage. But what I think doesn't matter. We need proof."

"Does that mean we're going to see her?"

He peered down his nose at me. "*We*? Oh, did you want to come along?"

Great. I was going to be punished for running off to the strip club while leaving him with Zach. "You need me," I said. "A man and a woman together are much less threatening than a man alone."

"What makes you think I want to be nonthreatening? Sometimes threats accomplish a lot."

"I'll make you something chocolate and yummy," I promised.

I knew that would get him. He had to sulk for a couple more minutes just to save face, but then he relented.

"Tomorrow morning we go in as insurance investigators looking into the death of her sister with regard to the policy benefits which will go to Lisa's next of kin. I spoke with Kristen earlier and made an appointment for nine o'clock."

"Can I have a cool name like Bubbles Galore this time?"

Fred scowled. "Good grief, no. You'll be Hilda Klapnauer, and I'll be Nathan Rivers. That's the names I gave Kristin, and I already have business cards printed."

"Hilda Klapnauer? Where do you come up with these names?"

"Where did you come up with Bubbles Galore?"

"Fine. I'm Hilda. Where are we going? Home? Business?"

"We're going to her apartment. Like her sister, she's an exotic dancer who works nights, and I don't think you need to visit any more strip clubs."

"Another stripper? What's her professional name?"

Fred cleared his throat and tilted his chin upward. "Tiger Lily," he said with as much dignity as possible.

"Tiger Lily. That's a nice name." I thought of Paula's description of the woman who'd visited her. "Is she tall and blonde with big boobs?"

"Her hair color varies from picture to picture, but it appears she is tall and amply endowed."

I sat forward excitedly. "Bingo! That's got to be her! Now if we can just verify that she has cat scratches, we'll know she was the one who broke into my house and visited Paula, and we can put a stop to these threats on my home and cat."

Fred looked suddenly serious. "Lindsay, we need to be cautious talking to this woman. Remember, she may be a murderer. She's been arrested in the past for everything from drunk and disorderly to prostitution."

"Wow. This should be interesting."

I saw no reason to mention that Trent knew about the sister and would likely be questioning her when he made it through all the official channels and rules and hoops he had to jump through. Fred and I were going to get there first.

***

I didn't sleep much during what was left of the night. My insomnia wasn't a result of worrying about Tiger Lily breaking into my house, whacking me over the head and stabbing me the way she'd done to Lisa. Now that the intruder had a name and was a real person, my fear had actually diminished. She was a woman, not a monster. I figured I had just as much of a chance to whack her with my iron skillet as she had to whack me with whatever she used on Lisa, especially since I had a vicious guard cat on my side.

My insomnia was caused partly by anticipation of finally meeting this woman and confronting her and partly by anticipation of getting there before Trent and sneering at him later for the way he tried to keep me out of the loop.

Fred had made a half-hearted attempt to get me to stay at his house for the night or let him sleep on my sofa, but it was pretty easy to dissuade him in his

233

Zach-weakened condition. I assured him Henry would alert me if there was a problem. I asked him if I could borrow the machine gun, but he refused. Men can be so selfish with their toys.

Henry wasn't happy with my restless night. He was already in a snit because I needed him to be alert and refused to give him catnip. Henry had the catnip monkey on his back. About the third time I woke, got up to go to the bathroom then flopped around for a while before going back to sleep, he gave an indignant snarl and jumped off the bed to sleep on the floor.

I had finally drifted into a sound sleep when the alarm I'd forgotten to reset went off at 4:00. With cat-like reflexes, I rolled out of bed, grabbed the skillet from my nightstand and looked around for someone to whack. Henry opened one blue eye, looked disgusted, closed that eye and went back to sleep.

I tried to do the same, but I was really wired by that time so I got up and had some eggs with cheese, a Coke and a few cookies for breakfast. Henry ate his breakfast then demanded to go outside. I let him since he was in a really grumpy mood, and I figured Tiger Lily would not be up and roaming around at that hour after a long night of dancing around a pole and inhaling stale cigarette smoke.

I made a pan of brownies (for purposes of bribery with Fred and Trent), did my dishes, tidied up my kitchen, sorted my chocolate chips according to size and percentage of chocolate, straightened my pictures, sharpened my knives, started my laundry and finally called Fred.

"I assume you're being held at gunpoint," he said. "That's the only thing that can justify calling me at this hour." But he sounded wide awake.

"The sun's almost up," I said. "I can't sleep. Let's go roust out Tiger Lily, take her by surprise." Get there before Trent.

"Go back to bed and call me after the sun rises."

"I have fresh chocolate brownies, just the way you like them, with nuts. Still warm. I've got vanilla bean ice cream to go with them."

Fred sighed, but I knew I had him. "Put on your black suit with a white shirt and low heels, and I'll be at your place before the brownies get cold, but remember, our appointment isn't until nine."

Fifteen minutes later he was at my door carrying his own cup of coffee and looking quite spiffy in a pin-striped gray suit and dark red tie. I felt that I looked professional in my trusty black suit, but not actually well-dressed and sophisticated like Fred. Maybe I ought to invest in another sedate outfit. However, I had nowhere to wear it except on these expeditions with Fred and to the occasional funeral.

We sat around eating and drinking for a while, then at eight o'clock I finally persuaded him to leave, go to our appointment a few minutes early. It sounded like something an insurance investigator might do.

"Let me get Henry inside, and I'll be ready to leave." I stood on the porch and called him. Usually when I do that, he comes loping in, pretending he was already on his way home when he heard me call because cats don't answer to anybody. That morning he didn't appear.

Fred came up behind me. "Do you want to hang around here until he shows up?"

I shook my head. "He's probably hiding in a bush, watching me and laughing. He wasn't very happy when he left this morning. We won't be gone long. If he has to wait for me when he's finally ready to go inside, maybe it'll teach him to come when I call."

I didn't like going off and leaving him outside, but in the few months I'd been owned by a cat, I'd learned a lot about them. The number one lesson was that cats will do what they please, and those of us who love them must accept that and learn to live with it. Not a bad lesson to learn about relationships in general, I supposed. Trent needed to learn that lesson.

Fred and I set off for Tiger Lily's apartment shortly after eight.

She lived in an older building in an older part of town. Not the best area, but not the worst, either. However, Fred's pristine vintage Mercedes did look a little out of place parked at the curb.

"Are you packing heat?" I asked as we walked up the cracked sidewalk toward the red brick structure that also had a few cracks.

He shook his head and continued walking. "You watch too much television."

"Define *too much*."

"Whatever amount you watch. I don't need a gun. We're simply paying a visit to a woman."

"Yeah, a woman who killed her sister."

I made a mental note to look into getting my right to carry when this was over. An iron skillet was a good weapon, but I'd have to get up close and personal to use it. I could fire a gun from across the room. There was a reason cops carried guns instead of iron skillets.

Fred opened the door, and we entered the building. Again I was met with the overpowering smell of stale cigarette smoke, but this time scents of bacon, cabbage and various other foods mingled and lingered. Four wooden doors with metal numbers sat along the hallway.

"Upstairs," Fred instructed, pointing in the direction of a battered wooden staircase. "Fourth floor."

"Fourth floor? How about we take the elevator?"

"Very funny. Let's go."

When we finally made it to the fourth floor, I stopped and turned to Fred. "Don't let her kick you. That woman has got to have strong legs if she makes it up these stairs every day."

"Apartment 4B," he said, pointing to the door on the right.

We walked over and knocked.

And knocked.

"Sleeps pretty sound," I said.

Fred took out his cell phone and punched in a number. A phone inside the apartment began to ring.

And ring.

Fred disconnected the call. "We're early. We'll wait."

"Fifteen minutes early. Big deal. She ought to be up and at least in the shower by now."

Fifteen minutes passed.

Thirty.

"I think you've been stood up," I said. "Maybe you were too threatening."

"I told her there might be money in it for her. That usually works."

I studied the door. In addition to the ancient lock which, according to the TV shows I watched, I could open with a credit card, it also had a much sturdier looking deadbolt. "I'll take care of the bottom one if you can open the top," I offered.

"What are you suggesting, that we break in?"

"Oh, like you've never done that before?"

"We need to go home and regroup."

I sighed in disappointment. "I guess so. Henry's probably ready to come in by now." We started trudging back down the stairs. "I wonder if Trent got here early and arrested her."

"Was he planning to arrest her today?"

"I have no idea. Nobody tells me anything."

"I'll check when we get home."

"And you'll let me know?"

"Of course."

I was very much afraid Trent had beaten me to the punch on Tiger Lily. Damn. I hated to lose, but at the same time I felt an immense relief at the thought that neither my cat nor I would be threatened that night. I would never again take for granted the feeling of safety and security when I locked my doors at night and went to bed.

And I was definitely going to look into taking those gun classes. A machine gun like the one Fred had would go a long way toward restoring my sense of safety and security.

\*\*\*

Henry was not waiting when I got home. An ugly little worry niggled as I climbed the steps to my front porch. I told myself I was being silly. Henry had been on his own when he came to live with me. He could take care of himself. In the less than a year he'd lived with me, he'd terrorized all the cats in the neighborhood and most of the dogs, even the big ones. Especially the big ones.

I went upstairs to change into something comfortable. The sun blazed out of the clear blue sky without a cloud in sight. It was going to be another cut-offs and tee-shirt day. As I changed clothes, I thought about what I was going to do for the rest of the day. I'd spent most of my time at the restaurant for so long, I had no idea what to do with spare time.

Maybe Fred and I could make another trip to Tiger Lily's place that afternoon.

Maybe I'd take Henry to the park when he got back. Find him some new cats and dogs to terrorize.

I smiled to myself as I went back downstairs. He'd enjoy that, maybe forgive me for the bad night.

I reached the bottom of the stairs and turned into my living room.

"Lindsay Powell, we finally meet." A tall blonde woman dressed in a pair of minimal shorts and a tube top that emphasized her huge boobs stood in the middle of my living room holding an enormous gun.

Okay, the gun was a pistol, not even close to the size of Fred's machine gun, but that barrel pointed in my direction was way too big for my comfort.

# Chapter Twenty-Three

I swallowed hard. To be more precise, I gulped. To be totally honest, I almost peed my pants.

"Who—?" I said in a whisper. It was the best I could do under the circumstances.

"I think you know who I am. You and your cop friend made that bogus appointment to see me this morning. Like I'd believe that bitch Lisa would leave me any insurance money." She snorted and waved her gun toward my recliner. "Sit down."

I didn't bother to correct her that it was Fred, not Trent, who'd made the bogus appointment with her. At that point, I didn't think it made much difference. I just stumbled obediently in the direction she indicated.

On the far side of the coffee table I saw a pet carrier with an unmoving white animal inside.

My heart stopped and I dropped to my knees, oblivious of guns and anti-aircraft or any other weapons that evil woman might have. "Henry!" I fumbled with the latch on the door.

"Don't open that! Your cat's okay. I'd never hurt an animal. You think I'm some kind of a monster?"

Actually, I did, but thought it best to keep my mouth shut for once in my life.

241

"Get up," she ordered. "Leave him in the cage so I don't have to hurt him."

"He's not moving!"

"He's just asleep. I lured him into that cage with catnip. He'll come out of it in a couple of hours." She rubbed her free hand over her arm, and I saw the healing evidence of cat scratches. Yay, Henry!

I reached a finger through the wire mesh of the door and stroked him. "Henry?"

He lifted his head, opened his eyes, purred and lay back down.

When this was over, we were going to have a talk about his addiction.

If we both survived.

"Get up off the floor," Tiger Lily ordered. "Sit in that chair. We got some business to take care of."

I obeyed. That gun accomplished what Trent, Rick and even my parents had been unable to accomplish. I did exactly as the woman ordered.

"You've got something of mine," she said.

"Your earring? Whatever it is, you can have it back."

She smiled. Well, her lips curved upward, but it wasn't the kind of smile I was accustomed to seeing when someone bit into one of my chocolate chip cookies. "I'm glad you're going to be reasonable. Just give me my ten million dollars, and everybody will be happy."

Somehow I didn't quite believe her. If I had the money and gave it to her, I suspected she'd still kill me so I couldn't tell on her.

"If I had the money, I'd give it to you. I don't have it. Somebody got to it before you."

"Yeah, I know somebody did. It wasn't Lisa, so that leaves you."

My stomach clenched into a hard little knot. "You really did kill your own sister?"

She grimaced and waved the gun through the air. "She was not my sister! She was my mother's third husband's daughter."

"Your step sister."

"Call her whatever you want. She was a bitch, a spoiled bitch. She was two years younger than me...two freaking years! But she was the baby. We always had to take care of poor little Lisa."

I cringed as she echoed the very words Rick had used about the woman. "She wasn't all that little," I said, hoping that would somehow be conciliatory.

But Tiger Lily continued to rant and wave the gun around. Obviously Lisa was a sore spot for her. "Poor little Lisa got a new dress whenever she wanted one, but I had to work for my clothes! Poor little Lisa had the same last name as everybody else in the family, everybody but me. Poor little Lisa had every guy in the neighborhood on her string. Poor little Lisa got the trailer when our parents died because her daddy owned it, not my mother. Poor little Lisa thought she was going to be rich, but I took George away from her, and I'm going to get the money!"

"George loved you, not her." Surely that was something she wanted to hear, something that would calm her.

She looked down at me, her expression a little closer to happy than it was before. The hand holding the gun dropped to her side. "Yes, he did. He was going to run away with me, not her. But then she turned him in." She straightened, lifting the gun to point directly at me again. There was no longer any sign of happy on her face. Her mouth settled into a thin line.

"That was a terrible thing for her to do," I said sympathetically, "betraying him like that, sending him to prison just so you couldn't have him."

"George knew I'd wait for him until he got out, but that bitch got Rodney Bradford to betray George's trust, and they were going to steal our money."

"They were bad people." I was making every effort I could think of to become her new best friend.

She nodded. "They were. When George heard he married Lisa, he knew what they were up to. He told me where to find the money so I could get it before they did. He trusted me. Bradford only knew it was somewhere in your house. They had to get your house and tear it down to find the money." Her scowl deepened. "That damned husband of yours was helping them."

I heard a low growl and looked down to see Henry's paw groping with the latch on his cage. He was finally sobering up and not happy about being confined. His cage was behind Tiger Lily, so she didn't see him. I lifted my eyes quickly before she noticed and followed the direction of my gaze. If

Henry could get out, between the two of us, we might be able to take her.

Okay, Henry would be able to take her, and I'd stand back and watch. He'd already run her off a couple of times without my help.

"But they didn't get the money," I said, talking loudly so she wouldn't hear Henry grumbling and jiggling that latch. "Rodney died. Someone poisoned him, someone much cleverer than Lisa." I tried to smile. "Someone like you."

She shrugged, and looked proud. "Getting rid of Bradford was easy. He always stopped at the same place for coffee because poor little Lisa couldn't make decent coffee. Never had to learn. Somebody always did it for her. So I just waited for Bradford to show up, sat down at his table, got him to talking and looking at my boobs, and dropped in some ground up amoprine berries I got from his old girlfriend's tree."

Henry almost lifted the latch. He'd get it eventually if I could stay alive until then. Tiger Lily liked flattery. I'd better pour on some more of that.

"You sent him the text message asking him to come by Dorothy's place so she'd be blamed. Smart. But did you know he was only leading Lisa on? He planned to dump her and go back to Dorothy once they got the money."

Tiger Lily smiled for real that time. "I wish I'd known that so I could have told her before she died. George didn't love her, and Bradford didn't love her either."

"George loved you. You stole him from Lisa. You're the only one he trusted with the location of his money."

"That's right. He knows I'll keep it safe for him until he gets out of prison. Then we're going to get a big house and a new car." Her eyes narrowed. "You need to give it to me now. I killed Rodney Bradford and that bitch Lisa to keep them from getting it. Don't think for one minute I won't kill you too."

I shifted uneasily in the chair. "Yeah, I believe you. But I don't have your money. Somebody broke in here and dug up the basement right after Bradford was killed."

She frowned.

"They did, I swear. I don't know how they got in, but they did, and when I got down there, somebody had already been digging around."

She shook her head. "That was me. I came in through the coal chute, just like George did when he was a teenager and his stuffy grandparents didn't want him to go out at night. He told me where the padlock key was hidden, and I got right in. I dug around where George told me to dig, but there was no money." She centered the gun barrel on my forehead. "That means you found it first."

I blinked and flinched backward. "You talked to Paula. You found out from her that I haven't come into any huge amounts of money."

"She's your friend. I don't trust what she told me."

I was right. That had been her driving George's car. "George gave you his car, didn't he? You, not Lisa."

She nodded. "He trusts me with his car and his money. He loves me."

"That was you wearing the coat and hood and driving his car the evening you thought we were gone but we were just behind the house having a barbecue."

Her lips thinned. "That was me. I was trying to get inside to search. I came back once, and that damned cat of yours attacked me." She rubbed her arm again.

That damned cat of mine rattled the cage door and growled, his paw successfully lifting the latch and pushing the cage door open.

I cleared my throat to hide his noises and his escape, give him a chance to leap on her from behind and scratch out her eyes.

I caught a fleeting glimpse of him moving toward the kitchen. *The kitchen?* I was being threatened by a murderer, and my cat was going for a snack? Damn! Probably had the munchies from the catnip.

My heart sank. I was on my own.

"Maybe I know where your money is," I said.

Her eyes lit up. "Now you're getting smart. Where?"

"In my bedroom upstairs." If I could get her up there, maybe I could grab my iron skillet.

I rose and headed for the stairs. She was right behind me with that evil-looking gun. I was really going to have to get one of those when this was over. Actually, I needed to have one of those while this was going on.

Just as we crossed in front of the door, someone knocked.

Both Tiger Lily and I froze.

"Lindsay, it's me." *Trent.*

"My friend, the cop," I whispered, hoping the mention of a cop would scare her into leaving.

"Don't say anything," she instructed.

He knocked louder. "I know you're in there. I can see your car through the cracks in the garage. I'm not leaving until we talk about last night."

Tiger Lily smirked. "Have a problem with the boyfriend last night?"

"You have no idea."

"Tell him you'll talk to him later. Tell him to go away." She lowered the barrel of her gun to my right knee. "If you ever want to walk again, get rid of him."

I was quite fond of that knee and had high hopes of being able to walk again, but I had to try to get Trent to help.

"Go away," I shouted. "I haven't had my coffee yet, and you know I don't like to talk to anybody before I've had my coffee. I can't start the day without coffee."

He knew I never drank coffee, so he would surely realize I was sending him a coded message for help because someone was holding a gun on me and I couldn't talk except in code.

That was the way it worked on TV.

Trent heaved a deep sigh. "I get it." I hoped he did. "I understand you're mad because I can't share things with you like normal couples share things." He didn't get it. "We need to talk about this. You do things that worry me. You get yourself in situations where you could get hurt."

Yeah, like standing on the other side of the door with a crazy woman holding a gun to my knee.

"Go away, Adam." That would surely alert him that something was wrong. I never called him by his first name.

"Ouch. First-name basis? You really are mad at me. We need to talk."

My cat was a catnipaholic who'd deserted me for food, and my almost-boyfriend was being dense. I was totally on my own.

Tiger Lily nudged me with the barrel of the gun. "Get rid of him, now!" she whispered.

"I'll meet you at our favorite restaurant in two hours," I said. Since Death by Chocolate was my favorite restaurant, surely he'd figure that one out.

"Why are you standing on the porch, yelling at Lindsay?" Fred! Fred always knew everything that was going on. He'd doubtless come to rescue me because he had my house bugged and had heard every word Tiger Lily said. And even if he hadn't, he'd understand the coffee reference.

"Go away, both of you," I said. "Come back after I've had my morning coffee."

"Okay."

I was doomed. Even Fred didn't get it.

"Come on over to my place, Trent," he said. "I'll make you some good coffee in my Keurig."

My heart sank as I heard the two men leave my porch. If I survived this, they were both in so much trouble. Make that all three of them. Henry wasn't getting off lightly either.

Tiger Lily nudged me again. "Upstairs."

I dragged my feet climbing the stairs. No need to rush to my own death. I led her into my room and sidled over toward my nightstand.

"Where is it?"

"In there." I pointed to the stand.

She frowned. "In that little drawer? You didn't spend part of it, did you?" She lifted the gun with both hands.

"No! I didn't have time. It's all in there. It doesn't take up much room because it's in large bills."

"Get it out and give it to me."

Showtime.

I leaned over and pulled the drawer open with one hand while I grabbed my iron skillet with the other. I swung the skillet blindly, knowing I had only one slim chance to get out of this alive.

The skillet hit something with a clang and bounced out of my hand.

A gunshot screamed past my ear, *past* being the key word, not *into*.

I was still alive.

But so was Tiger Lily. I'd hit the gun, knocking it out of her hand, but she was scrambling to retrieve it.

I threw myself on the floor, trying to get to it before she did. I had my fingers on the barrel when she grabbed the handle and snatched it away, rising to her feet almost gracefully. Damned dancer. She did have muscular legs.

"You're dead." She stood in the doorway, raising that ugly gun and aiming it straight at me.

She didn't see the head of white hair that appeared out of nowhere behind her.

"Drop the gun!" Trent shouted just as one of Fred's arms grabbed the hand that held that gun and twisted it behind her back while the other wrapped around her neck.

Henry strolled into the room, sauntered over to where I sat in the floor and butted my hand.

My heroes.

# Chapter Twenty-Four

Tiger Lily did not go down easily. She shouted, screamed and struggled while Fred held her and Trent handcuffed her. I learned some new words that day, words I would have to be careful not to add to Zach's vocabulary.

"She's got my money!" the woman shrieked as Trent hauled her out of the room. "You *******  ****! That money doesn't belong to you! George told me where to find it, only me! Make her give it to me!"

"I'll call you later, Lindsay!" Trent shouted, trying to make himself heard over Tiger Lily's raving.

"Let me go! You don't have any right to do this to me! I just want what's mine!"

Fred crossed the room and offered a hand to help me up. Naturally I declined. I gave Henry one last hug, got to my feet and threw my arms around Fred.

I'd thought I might never see my cat, my friend or my future boyfriend again in this life. I couldn't get enough of touching the cat and the friend and assuring myself they were real and I was alive. As soon as Trent got back, I was going to hug him for a very long time too, maybe even forgive him for not keeping me in the loop.

Like Henry, Fred permitted me a brief hug, then pulled back and looked at me. The concern in his eyes was as warming as a hug. "Are you okay?" he asked. "Did she hurt you?"

I shook my head. "Other than aging twenty years in the last few minutes, I'm fine. That woman is seriously nuts!"

The outside door closed, and the sounds of Tiger Lily's rants diminished.

"A little borderline personality disorder," Fred speculated." I don't know how serious it is."

"If you'd been on the same end of that gun as I was, you'd know how serious it is!"

"I'm sure that would make a difference in perception."

I picked up Henry. "Let's go downstairs and get some Coke and chocolate."

We went down to the kitchen. My back door was standing open, hanging lopsidedly from one hinge, letting the cool air out and the hot air in.

Fred straightened it as much as possible. "You'll have to have it replaced. Looks like she took an axe to it. Apparently she got more and more angry with every failed attempt to get her hands on that money."

I shivered, set Henry on the floor and popped open fresh Cokes for Fred and me.

"Thank goodness you heard Trent and me yelling and came over to investigate," I said.

Fred accepted the soft drink. "I was already on my way to your house when I heard you and Trent yelling. My first clue was when Henry came to my back door, made a horrible noise and ripped my screen to shreds. Those claws are lethal."

I sank to the floor and hugged Henry again. He purred. "So you weren't deserting me. You just went for help. Good boy."

Fred snorted. "He probably thought I had more catnip."

At the mention of the magic word, Henry became instantly alert and strode over to his dish, looking back at me, his supplier. "Forget it," I said. "You can have some nice stinky tuna. I think you've had enough catnip for a while."

I opened a can of tuna and dumped half of it in Henry's bowl.

"I can't believe neither one of you understood my references to coffee which you know I never drink! I was trying to give you a code meaning somebody was holding a gun to my head and I needed help."

Fred pulled out a kitchen chair and sat in it. "Oh, that. Trent just thought you were being sarcastic, like saying you'd as soon drink coffee as talk to him. You must admit, you do the sarcasm thing a lot. I thought that reference might be a signal for help, but I already knew you were in trouble from Henry's actions and the fact that your back door was standing wide open. Did you fail to understand my reference to taking Trent to my place for a decent cup of coffee from my Keurig?"

I sat down in the chair beside him. "Your reference? I just thought you were going to make

Trent a cup of coffee to calm him down. I didn't even know you owned a Keurig."

He rolled his eyes. "I don't. You know I always grind my own coffee. I said that so you'd know I picked up on your coffee reference and would be coming in the back door to help you."

"You thought I'd get all that from your saying you were going to make Trent coffee in your Keurig?"

"No more bizarre than your thinking Trent would know you had a gun to your head when you said you needed coffee."

I couldn't argue with that logic. "Want a brownie?"

"Yes."

I got chocolate for both of us, sat back down and ate one. I was beginning to calm after my harrowing experience. "We know most of the answers. Kristen killed Lisa and Bradford, broke in here twice and tried a third time, questioned Paula, trying to find out if I had become suddenly rich so she'd know if I had the money. Rick said Lisa tried to burn down Death by Chocolate. But we still don't know who's got the money."

Fred drummed his fingers on the wooden table top and looked thoughtful. "I think I know, but I'm not certain."

"Amazing. There's something Fred Sommers doesn't know?"

"I plan to be certain in the near future."

"Rick and I did have an elderly couple renting this place between the time we bought it from the

Murrays and the time I moved in. Maybe they found it."

"I don't think so. They both had hip and knee problems. I doubt if they ever went downstairs. Anyway, when they left here, they moved in with their son across town, and nobody in that family has ten million dollars."

"Yeah, I didn't think it was them," I said, trying to save face.

"Perhaps the money never existed. Perhaps George's scheme to steal it failed, but he claimed to have the money to impress Kristen."

"Really?"

"I doubt it. But I refuse to speculate further until I have all the data."

"Yeah, well, I refuse to give you any more brownies until you speculate."

Fred thought about that for a moment. "I don't believe you," he said, reaching for a second brownie.

He was right. I would never deny a friend chocolate, especially not when that friend had just saved my life.

\*\*\*

Trent got Kristen Delaney booked for double homicide as well as breaking and entering. There was some question as to whether she alone was guilty of murder or whether George Murray was involved. He claimed he'd only told her to get the money and hide it from his duplicitous friend and former lover, Lisa, that the murders were the product of Kristen's own anger.

I didn't care what charges they brought against him. I was just happy that my home, cat and person were no longer threatened by a crazy woman.

Saturday morning Paula and I inspected Death by Chocolate. The company we'd hired did a great job of cleaning and repainting. We did some final clean-up and got everything ready to reopen on Monday morning. Life was returning to normal.

That afternoon the Murrays arrived just at seven for a cookout. Fred and Trent were already in the back yard discussing the relative merits of gas vs. charcoal grills, beer as a marinade for steaks and other things that guys can discuss all day without ever reaching a conclusion. Paula was still at home preparing twice-baked potatoes and a salad while Zach had his nap so he'd be ready to stay up half the night and learn some new swear words courtesy of Tiger Lily if I had too much wine.

I invited the Murrays inside and held my breath as they looked around, uncertain how they'd take my changes to their home. I hadn't made a lot of changes. I'd repainted so the walls were bright white, removed the heavy drapes and put up wooden mini-blinds. The hardwood floors were the same, and my furniture, while it was different from theirs, was antique or at least garage-sale-antique.

Cathy Murray moved around the room, touching the old sewing machine that had been my grandmother's, studying the drop-leaf table, also from my grandmother, that held a Tiffany-style lamp created just for me by my friend Alex. Harold and I stood at the door and watched her. Finally she came back, her eyes misty, and hugged me.

"It's beautiful," she said. "You've made a home here where we once had a home. I'm so glad the old place is still loved."

I relaxed and smiled. "I do love this place, and I'm so glad you approve of what I've done with it. Now that—" I flinched, realizing I'd been about to say something that might upset them since it involved their grandson.

Cathy patted my hand. "Now that nobody's trying to take it away from you, you can relax and enjoy it."

"I'm sorry about George. Looks like he may be in prison longer than you thought."

Harold wrapped an arm around his wife's waist and held her close. "George has made some bad choices, but I don't think he was involved in the murders. We've hired an attorney for him."

"Well, good. Trent says he probably won't be charged with theft since the crime was never reported. Not like a drug dealer's going to go running to the cops when he's been robbed. In fact, Fred's not a hundred percent certain the money ever existed."

Cathy brightened. "I'll bet you're right about that money. George always was a fanciful boy."

"She means he told a lot of lies," Harold said.

"Harold!"

"Let's go out back and get something to drink," I said. "I have plenty of soft drinks, and Fred always brings excellent wine. And you can meet Trent."

\*\*\*

The evening was a total success. The food was great, the conversation was fun, everybody got on well with everybody else. Zach and Henry chased lightning bugs with no fears. Zach crashed shortly after nine, and Paula left to take him home. Cathy and Harold stayed another hour then said they needed to get home too. Harold had an early tee-time.

I gave them a to-go bag with Oatmeal Fudge Sandwich cookies, then Fred, Trent and I walked with them to the front porch. The night had cooled quite nicely, and a full moon overhead cast intriguing shadows that changed my mundane yard to a fantasy world. Crickets chirped from their hiding places, and a bird rustled somewhere in my vast foliage. Henry slipped past me and disappeared into the bushes.

"Thank you for a wonderful evening," Cathy said, hugging everybody. "Next time will be at our place."

"I'm ready any time," I said.

Harold shook hands with Trent and Fred, then he gave me a hug.

They started off the porch, but Cathy turned back. "Oh, I must be getting senile! I left that bag of cookies you gave me sitting on your table. Trent, would you mind getting it for me?"

"Sure, no problem."

As soon as he left, Harold and Cathy moved closer. "We need to ask you something, Fred," Harold whispered.

"It's about the money," Cathy said.

Fred nodded. He didn't look confused. I found that very confusing.

259

"You have it, don't you?" Fred asked.

They both nodded. "We found it shortly after George was arrested," Cathy admitted. "He didn't hide it very well. That much money left quite a mound, and the bricks were all out of place."

"We put it in an account in the Cayman Islands," Harold said. "It's all still there. We just used the interest to pay George's attorney fees."

"And to pay back our retirement fund for some of the money we've given him over the years," Cathy said. "Do you think we're going to get in trouble? Should we give it back?"

Fred shook his head. "Who would you give it back to? You haven't committed any crime."

Harold nodded. "Good. We'll use it to help George start a new career when he gets out of prison."

"We're encouraging him to get his GED while he's still inside, then he can start college as soon as he gets out."

"Good plan," I said.

Trent opened the door and stepped out to join us. "I can't find that bag of cookies anywhere."

"Oh, silly me! I have it right here!" Cathy laughed and held up the bag.

Fred, Trent and I stood on the porch and waved as the Murrays drove away.

"Nice people," Trent said, "but what did she want to talk to you about when she sent me for a bag of cookies she knew she had all the time?"

I looked at Fred.

"Good night," he said and walked across the yard toward his house, deserting me.

"Well?" Trent asked.

Why couldn't he be as dense about Cathy's little deceit as he'd been about my attempt to send a coded message using *coffee*?

"She told us about a beautiful trip they took to the Cayman Islands," I said, wrapped my arms around him and kissed him. If that failed to distract him, I'd offer him more chocolate.

THE END

Check out some of Lindsay's favorite recipes on the following pages then read on for the first chapter of THE GREAT CHOCOLATE SCAM, the next book of Lindsay's ongoing adventures.

# Triple Chocolate Cake
(Thanks to my Beta Sigma Phi sister, Sandy
Bell, for sharing this recipe!)

1 pkg. dark or devil's food chocolate cake mix
3 oz. pkg. instant chocolate pudding mix
1/2 c. vegetable oil
1/2 c. Godiva Chocolate Liqueur (Sandy uses coffee,
but Lindsay doesn't like coffee)
10 oz. sour cream
12 oz. pkg. chocolate chips
4 eggs

Mix all ingredients except chocolate chips for
five minutes. Add chips. Pour into Bundt or tube pan
that has been greased and dusted with cocoa powder.
Bake for 65 minutes at 350 degrees. Cool at least
thirty minutes. Invert onto cake platter.

When totally cooled, sift powdered sugar on top
for color. This cake is moist and rich and does not
need frosting, but a scoop of vanilla bean ice cream
makes a very nice complement.

# Chocolate Mousse
(Thanks to my Beta Sigma Phi sister, Julia
Gibson, for sharing this recipe!)

12 oz. pkg. chocolate chips
1 lb. cream cheese
2 c. whipping cream
3/4 c. sugar
2 tsp. vanilla
Strawberries

Melt package of chocolate chips on low heat. Stir
well then set on counter to cool. Combine cream
cheese, sugar, salt, and vanilla with electric mixer.
Add melted chocolate and stir until everything is
blended and smooth again.

Beat whipping cream till peaks form and then
fold into chocolate mixture. Keep folding and
blending softly until totally mixed.

Pour this into pretty glasses and top with more
whipped cream and/or a strawberry.

# Triple Chocolate Chip Cookies with Chopped Hazelnuts

1/2 c. butter, softened
1-1/2 c. brown sugar
1 egg
1 T. vanilla
1/2 t. baking soda
dash of salt (bigger dash if you use unsalted butter)
1-1/2 c. flour
1/4 c. finely ground hazelnuts
1/4 c. oat flour
big handful semi-sweet chocolate chips
big handful white chocolate chips
big handful bittersweet chips (60% or more cacao)
1/2 to 1 c. chopped pecans (or other nuts)

Cream butter with sugar. Add egg and vanilla and stir determinedly until well mixed. Combine dry ingredients and add to butter mixture. Stir in chocolate chips and nuts. Dough should be very stiff and just a tiny bit sticky. Add more flour (wheat, oat or nut) or butter as necessary to achieve this state.

Form dough into balls the size of small golf-balls and lay on cookie sheet. Bake at 375° for 8 minutes (more if you prefer a crisp cookie).

Makes approximately 2 dozen cookies, depending on how many samples were tested before baking.

# Gluten-Free Chocolate Chip Cookies

1/2 c. butter, softened
1-1/2 c. brown sugar
1 egg
1 T. vanilla
1/2 t. baking soda
dash of salt (bigger dash if you use unsalted butter)
1-3/4 c. rice flour
1/3 c. potato starch
2 T. tapioca flour
1/4 c. oat flour
big handful semi-sweet chocolate chips
big handful white chocolate chips
big handful bittersweet chips (60% or more cacao)
1/2 to 1 c. chopped pecans (or other nuts)

Cream butter with sugar. Add egg and vanilla and stir determinedly until well mixed. Combine dry ingredients and add to butter mixture. Stir in chocolate chips and nuts. Dough should be very stiff and just a tiny bit sticky. Add more flour (rice or oat) or butter as necessary to achieve this state.

Form dough into balls the size of small golf-balls and lay on cookie sheet. Bake at 375° for 8 minutes (more if you prefer a crisp cookie).

Makes approximately 2 dozen cookies, depending on how many samples were tested before baking.

# Killer Chocolate (aka Murdered Man's Brownies)

1/2 c. butter
3 squares unsweetened chocolate
1 c. sugar
2 eggs
2 t. vanilla
1/2 c. flour
dash of salt
1/2 c. chopped nuts
handful semi-sweet chocolate chips
handful white chocolate chips
handful bittersweet chips (60% or more cacao)

Melt butter and chocolate in microwave. Set aside to cool. Beat sugar, eggs and vanilla. Add cooled chocolate/butter combination and stir until well mixed. Add flour and stir until well mixed. Add nuts and chips. Bake in 8 or 9 inch square pan, greased and dusted with cocoa, at 350 degrees for thirty minutes.

Serve warm with vanilla bean ice cream or cool and frost, then toss a few more chocolate chips on top.

## Chocolate Frosting for Killer Chocolate Brownies

1 4-oz pkg. cream cheese, room temperature
1/4 c. butter, room temperature
1/4 c. unsweetened cocoa powder
2 c. powdered sugar
1 t. vanilla

Stir cocoa into part of the powdered sugar and set aside. Beat cream cheese and butter until smooth. Add powdered sugar, including the powdered sugar mixed with cocoa, and beat until smooth. Add vanilla and beat some more.

# Chocolate Cupcakes with Cream Cheese Filling

Filling:
1 8-oz. pkg. cream cheese, room temperature
1 egg
1/3 c. sugar
dash of salt

Beat cream cheese, egg, sugar and salt. Set aside.

Cupcakes:
3 c. flour
1/2 c. cocoa
2 c. sugar
1/2 t. salt
2 t. baking soda
2/3 c. oil
2 c. water
2 t. vanilla
2 T. vinegar

Stir together flour, cocoa, sugar, salt and baking soda. Add oil, water, vanilla and vinegar. Blend just until smooth.

Put cupcake liners in muffin pans. Fill each liner 2/3 full of batter. Top with a heaping teaspoonful of cream cheese mixture. Bake at 350 degrees for 20 minutes.

# Chocolate Fudge with Peanut Butter

2/3 c. cocoa
3 c. sugar
dash of salt
1 c. milk or cream
2 T. butter
2 t. vanilla
1/2 c. peanut butter

Mix sugar, salt and cocoa in saucepan. Stir in milk. Bring to a moderate boil over medium heat, stirring constantly. Cook to soft ball stage (234 degrees). Remove from heat. Add butter and vanilla. Cool until mixture is warm but not hot. Beat until thick and glossy. Quickly add peanut butter and swirl through. Pour into buttered 8 or 9 inch square pan.

# Oatmeal Fudge Sandwich Cookies

2/3 c. butter
2 c. oats
1 c. sugar
2/3 c. flour
1/4 light corn syrup
1/4 c. milk
2 t. vanilla
Dash of salt
12 oz. pkg. semi-sweet chocolate chips

Melt butter. Stir in oats, sugar, flour, corn syrup, milk and vanilla. Drop by spoonsful onto cookie sheet, far enough apart to be able to spread cookie mixture thin. Bake 6 to 8 minutes at 375 degrees. Cool completely and remove carefully.

Melt chocolate chips and spread on half of cookies. Put other half of cookies on top to make sandwich.

# Chocolate Marble Cheesecake

**Crust:**
1-1/2 c. vanilla wafer crumbs (about 45 wafers, crushed)
1/2 c. powdered sugar
1/3 c. cocoa
1/3 c. melted butter

Mix and press onto bottom of 9-inch springform pan.

**Cheesecake:**
3 8-oz. pkgs. cream cheese, room temperature
1 can sweetened condensed milk
3 eggs
1 T. vanilla
2 squares unsweetened chocolate, melted

Mix cream cheese and sweetened, condensed milk and beat until smooth. Add eggs and vanilla. Mix well. Pour half the batter over prepared crust.
Stir melted chocolate into remaining batter. Spoon over vanilla batter. Using knife or spatula, gently swirl chocolate batter through vanilla batter to marble.
Bake 50 minutes at 300 degrees.

# THE GREAT CHOCOLATE SCAM

## Chapter One

I sat in the client chair in my lawyer's office, tapping my foot and fidgeting. Rick was fifteen minutes late for our appointment to sign the divorce papers.

Based on the last year and a half of his alternating between *I want a divorce* and *I want you back*, I suppose I shouldn't have been surprised. But this time he'd seemed desperate to get it done as soon as possible. In fact, he was disappointed we had to wait a week for our attorneys to find a mutually available time to get together.

I figured he was in love again. He hadn't said so, but that was usually the reason he was ready to sign off on the divorce. Rick fell in love regularly. He fell out just as quickly, but that would soon no longer be my problem.

I was looking forward to being a free woman with no more ties to Rick-head, to owning one hundred percent of my little restaurant, Death by Chocolate, and to dating Detective Adam Trent officially. Soon Rick couldn't show up at my front door with protestations of eternal love or plans for some barely-legal scheme that somehow involved me. Well, he could still show up and try to involve me, but he wouldn't be able to use the lever of

1

signing the divorce papers to get me to aid and abet him.

I had even bought a new outfit to wear to my lawyer's office for the big event, a dark purple raw silk pantsuit with a turquoise and lavender scarf. Very elegant and stylish. My friend, Paula, went with me to pick it out. When clothing goes beyond blue jeans and tee-shirts, I'm lost.

So I sat there in the office of Jason Beckwirth of Hoskins, Grier, Morris and Beckwirth, looking elegant and stylish and irritated, waiting for my former knight in tarnished armor to show up and make me the happiest woman in the world by agreeing to unmarry me.

Why wasn't I waiting at my father's law firm? Because divorce is beneath them. They're corporate lawyers handling real estate deals, tax law, estate planning, that sort of *respectable* law. Besides that, he and Mom blamed me for the failure of a marriage they'd tried to prevent. After trashing him for years, suddenly when I announced I was divorcing Rick, he became their favorite son-in-law. I'm an only child, so that was really no great feat.

Jason looked up from the papers he was studying and smiled. He has a deceptively genial expression, looks like the boy next door, but he turns into the cut-throat lawyer next door in the courtroom. "Relax," he said. "They'll be here any minute. You know Rick will be late to his own funeral."

I crossed my legs and changed to swinging instead of tapping. "This waiting makes me nervous. I don't trust him."

Jason nodded. "With good reason. But when I talked to his lawyer last week, he said Rick was adamant about going through with this. You sure I can't get you a cup of coffee?"

"No, but a Coke would be good." I'd only had one so far that day. Our breakfast and lunch crowds at the restaurant were hectic and hungry, so Paula and I had been too busy to do much eating or drinking ourselves. My stomach rumbled and reminded me about the eating part.

Jason called his assistant, and she brought me a glass of Coke with ice. I preferred my Coke straight, no melting ice to dilute it, but at that moment, I would have settled for a Pepsi.

I finished the soft drink, swung my right leg then my left, tapped my feet, drummed my fingers and waited.

No Rick.

The beige phone on Jason's desk jangled—in a dignified manner, of course. Jason glanced at the display. "It's Bert," he said and lifted the receiver.

Bert Hanson, Rick's lawyer.

I inhaled sharply. I tried to tell myself he was probably calling to say they were stuck in traffic, but my heart sank down to the tip of my little toe. I had a horrible feeling Rick was jacking me around again. His lawyer was calling to say he'd cancelled.

I watched Jason's face, listened to every word he said, strained to hear the other side of the conversation. I couldn't, of course. My neighbor Fred probably could have if he'd been there. I'm pretty

3

sure Fred has super powers. Not that I've seen him flying or anything like that.

Yet.

Jason didn't say much. "I see." He looked at me and shook his head. That was a bad sign. "Okay. Well, thanks for letting me know."

He cradled the receiver, then lifted his gaze and folded his hands on his desk. "Lindsay—"

"He's not coming, is he?"

Jason sighed and shook his head. "It doesn't look like it. He didn't show up at Bert's office, and Bert hasn't been able to reach him by phone."

"Damn it!" I slammed my hand on the arm of the chair, shot up and spun around. I needed to go outside, run, hit something, eat huge quantities of chocolate. I needed to vent the anger that flared up inside me. This time I'd dared to hope. This time I really thought it was going to happen. This time the disappointment was even worse than usual.

I thought about the night on the town Trent and I had planned in celebration. The Divorcement Party I'd scheduled for Saturday night. None of it was going to happen. Rick was still causing problems, still controlling my life.

I stomped to one side of the room then back to the other, cursing with vehemence and sincerity. "Damn it, damn it, damn it! I knew it! That sorry, worthless, no-good—"

My cell phone began to play George Strait's *Blue Clear Sky*, Trent's ringtone.

"I'm sorry." I strode over to my purse and pulled out the phone to shut it off and send the call straight to voice mail, but then decided maybe I should answer and tell Trent I'd return his call in a couple of minutes. There was no reason for me to stay in Jason's office any longer. We weren't going to do business that day.

"Hi, Trent. Can I call you right back?"

"No."

"No?"

"I need to talk to you right now. I wanted you to hear this from me before you see it on television."

On television? No good news ever got reported on television. "Okay, fine, hang on and let me say good-bye to Jason. I'm just leaving my attorney's office. Rick was a no show."

"I know."

"You do?" Fred was the one who always knew things. Apparently Trent had just developed psychic abilities too.

"There's been an accident."

My insides went cold at that sentence, and I sank back down into my chair. The cops on TV said those words when they came to tell a family about a death. Images of the people I cared about most whirled through my mind. My parents, Fred, Paula, Zach, Henry… "What kind of accident? Who?"

He paused for what seemed like an hour but was probably closer to a second. "It's Rick. There was an explosion. His car was blown up in his driveway."

I frowned, relieved and puzzled. That explained why he hadn't shown up for our meeting. He'd have trouble driving if his car exploded. "An accident?

Rick's a terrible mechanic, but blowing up his own car seems like quite a feat even for him."

"He didn't blow it up. Somebody else did. Lindsay, you need to come down to the station."

"Why? Are you craving my chocolate chip cookies?" I was grasping at straws. I could tell from the somber tone of his voice that he wasn't trying to wheedle cookies.

"We need to ask you some questions." He paused again, and I could hear him draw in a deep breath. "Rick was in the car when it blew up. Lindsay, Rick's dead."

## About the Author:

I grew up in a small rural town in southeastern Oklahoma where our favorite entertainment on summer evenings was to sit outside under the stars and tell stories. When I went to bed at night, instead of a lullaby, I got a story. That could be due to the fact that everybody in my family has a singing voice like a bullfrog with laryngitis, but they sure could tell stories—ghost stories, funny stories, happy stories, scary stories.

For as long as I can remember I've been a storyteller. Thank goodness for computers so I can write down my stories. It's hard to make listeners sit still for the length of a book! Like my family's tales, my stories are funny, scary, dramatic, romantic, paranormal, magic.

Besides writing, my interests are reading, eating chocolate and riding my Harley.

Contact information is available on my website. I love to talk to readers! And writers. And riders. And computer programmers. Okay, I just plain love to talk!

http://www.sallyberneathy.com